# Look what people are saying about Betina Krahn...

"Ms. Krahn is truly ingenious....
You have to read her books!"
—*The Literary Times*

"One of the genre's most creative writers.
Her ingenious romances always entertain
and leave readers with a warm glow."
—*Romantic Times BOOKreviews*

"Wonderfully romantic...brilliantly written and
a joy to read...humorous, witty, and original...
Betina Krahn is talented and gifted. Her writing
is superb...perfectly charming."
—*The Literary Times*

"Merry, heart-charming...Betina Krahn
is a treasure among historical writers, and
*The Husband Test* is a story to savor."
—*BookPage*

"Witty, rollicking romance...Krahn's amusing
follow-up to *The Husband Test* quickly blossoms
into a bright, exciting adventure."
—*Publishers Weekly* on *The Wife Test*

"With *The Marriage Test*, Krahn has perfected
her unique recipe for highly amusing historical
romances as she deftly brings together two perfectly
matched protagonists to create a delectable
romance most readers will find impossible to resist."
—*Booklist* (starred review)

# Blaze

Dear Reader,

Welcome to my Harlequin Blaze debut! The minute I heard about Blaze Historicals, I was intrigued. Now, after writing my first book, Harlequin's vision for "big, sexy books in a smaller format" has me totally hooked. Some friends joked that I usually take 60,000 words to say hello! Well, eat those words, my friends; after writing 120,000-word books forever, I found this shorter format for a historical a dream come true!

Writing *Make Me Yours* was the most fun I'd had at the keyboard in years. The characters were so compelling, the story came so naturally and the tighter focus on "pure romance" was so freeing! My favorite heroines have always been gals with the gumption to go after what they want and a plan to get it. My favorite heroes are strong, stubborn men who think they know best, but get "taken to school" by a smart, sexy woman. I think I've been writing a Harlequin Blaze heroine for years without knowing it!

I'm hoping you enjoy Jack and Mariah and the Prince and Mercy. Come by my Web site afterward (BetinaKrahn.com) and let me know how you liked the way we're setting history a-BLAZE!

Happy reading!

Betina Krahn

New York Times Bestselling Author

# BETINA KRAHN

*Make Me Yours*

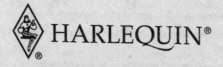

## HARLEQUIN®

TORONTO • NEW YORK • LONDON
AMSTERDAM • PARIS • SYDNEY • HAMBURG
STOCKHOLM • ATHENS • TOKYO • MILAN • MADRID
PRAGUE • WARSAW • BUDAPEST • AUCKLAND

Recycling programs
for this product may
not exist in your area.

ISBN-13: 978-0-373-79483-6

MAKE ME YOURS

www.eHarlequin.com

**Printed in U.S.A.**

## ABOUT THE AUTHOR

*New York Times* bestselling author Betina Krahn, mother of two and owner of two (humans and canines, respectively), shares the Florida sunshine with her fiancé and a fun and crazy sister. Her historical romances have received reviewer's choice and lifetime achievement awards and appear regularly on bestseller lists...including the coveted *USA TODAY* and *New York Times* lists.

Her books have been called "sexy," "warm," "witty" and even "wise." But the description that pleases her most is "funny"—because she believes the only thing the world needs as much as it needs love is laughter.

You can learn more about her books and contact her through her Web site, BetinaKrahn.com.

For Rex,
who always believes in me.

# 1

*England's Lake Country, 1887*

"ALL I WANT is to be left alone to run my own life and tend my business in peace. Is that too bloody much to ask?" Mariah Eller muttered as she pulled her cloak tighter against the wind-whipped rain and squinted, trying to make out the lights from the Eller-Stapleton Inn. There were at least a dozen things she'd rather be doing at nine o'clock on a rainy October evening…most involving a glowing fire and toasty slippers.

"Hurry, miz!" The boy with the lantern looked back anxiously and halted for her to catch up. "Pa said they wus about to blow the winders out."

"They'd better not touch my blessed windows," she declared, wishing the threat didn't sound so thin in her own ears. She motioned the boy forward on the darkened gravel path that led from her house to her inn. "That glazing cost me a fortune. I'm in hock up to my—" She pulled her icy hands inside her cloak. "If they lay one finger on that glass—"

She'd do what? Scold them? Send them to bed without supper? What could she possibly do to a group of men who were drinking, out of control and bent on destruction?

The sprawling Eller-Stapleton Inn, a coaching stop for travelers on the way north, was miles from the nearest town

and constable. Ordinarily she and her staff took care of their
own problems. Her capable innkeeper, Mr. Carson, main-
tained order with his razor-like glare, beefy arms and re-
doubtable old musket.

But something about this situation exceeded his unflappable grasp.

It must be bad indeed.

Taking a deep breath, she dashed the last few yards through
the puddles in the backyard and through the open kitchen door.
She stood for a moment taking her bearings, her long cloak
dripping water on the worn flagstone floor. The inn's staff was
collected around the glowing stone hearth at the far end of the
kitchen. They greeted her with "Thank the Lord, yer here"…all
but Carson, who seemed little relieved by her presence.

"Since when do you need help to deal with a few drunk
gentlemen?" she said, lowering her hood and wiping rain
from her face.

"The wretches grabbed Nell," Carson said, pointing to the
inn's cook and one of the serving women, who were huddled
with their arms around young Nell Jacoby. The little cham-
bermaid's face was as white as her eyes were red. "Kissed an'
groped her—acted like they meant to have her right on the
damned tabletop, fergive th' French."

His square, usually pleasant face burned dull crimson and
his blocky shoulders were thick with tension.

"Wild as March hares an' gettin' wilder. I'd 'ave bounced
the lot, except—" it clearly pained him to say "—I seen a crest
on one gent's snuffbox. And my boy says there be a coat o'
arms on the chase coach that brought their guns an' baggage."

*Noblemen.* Mariah groaned. *It would be.*

"Who are they? Did they not give names?" she asked,
hoping they had refused. By law, an inn's patrons had to
identify themselves and sign a register to obtain lodgings.

"They give names, all right." Carson glowered, reaching for his big leather register and opening it to the current page. "Jus' not their own."

"Jack Sprat and Jack B. Nimble," she read aloud. "Union Jack. Jack A. Dandy. Jack Ketch. Jack O. Lantern." She swallowed hard against the lump those names left in her throat. "Clever boys."

Worrisome boys, too, she realized. Giving no names meant taking no responsibility. Apparently they *did* intend to blow her windows out tonight.

Lord, how she hated titled men "gone a-hunting." Turned loose on a distant countryside, they felt free to vent every base impulse and indulge every low urge their otherwise "exemplary" lives denied them. When worse came to worst, as it often did, no mere innkeeper could manhandle them with impunity. Which left only the dicey art of diplomacy.

Dealing with powerful men behaving badly required a unique set of skills…sleight-of-hand, humor and whopping doses of honesty and flattery. It was like walking a tightrope. She looked at the apologetic expectation in Carson's face and her heart sank. She had no noble neighbor to call for help, no well-born husband to step in on her behalf. It was up to her. She was going to have to be very, very good on that tightrope tonight.

Removing her soggy cloak, she handed it off to Carson's son to hang by the door, then glanced down at what she wore. Her tailored navy woolen jacket, white blouse sans frills, and fitted gray wool skirt weren't exactly ideal for disarming drunken noblemen, but she had no time to change.

"I need a mirror, a fiddle player and a bottomless bowl of wassail—" her eyes glinted with the resentment she had to harness "—spiked with the strongest rum we've got."

Nodding with relief, Carson sent his son to fetch Old

Farley the stableman and his fiddle, then ordered the scullery maid to get a mirror from the staff living quarters. Bursts of raucous male laughter rolled down the passage from the public room, interspersed with the sounds of metal cups crashing on the floor, calls for more drink and howls for the innkeeper to "send that ripe little maid back out here."

Mariah looked at the faces turned her way and summoned all her determination. This was her business, her home, her life. Her people depended on her. She had to defend them with the only resources she had: her nerve and her wits.

The mirror arrived and she loosened and repinned her thick honey-colored hair into a freer style, removed her jacket and unbuttoned the blouse at her throat. She wasn't a great beauty, but her mercurial and exacting husband had often bragged that men turned to look at her a second time when she smiled. Running a finger over her teeth and pinching her cheeks, she checked the mirror. Her eyes shone with a confidence that surprised her.

"Stay awake, Carson, in case I should need you, and keep the drink coming." After downing a gulp of the brew being prepared for their guests, she picked up a bottle of her best rum and strode into the public room.

Her strategy was both simple and risky: find the leader, engage him and enlist his aid in keeping things under control while the lot drank themselves into harmless oblivion. If that failed, she'd scream bloody murder and Carson would come running with his faithful musket, Old Blunder.

Six men, mostly young, all well-dressed, were sprawled on benches and chairs around the flickering hearth at the far end of the inn's oak-paneled public room. There were no other patrons present, which was odd, given the miserable weather and the fact that the register showed every sleeping room in the inn was occupied. The men's behavior had apparently cleared the room.

At close range she could both see and smell their careless affluence. Glinting gold watch chains and Corinthian leather boots…sandalwood soap and brandy-flavored tobacco…muddied chairs and tables where they propped their feet…ash from their cigars on her polished floor…empty ale cups abandoned on table, floor and hearth.

"More to drink, gentlemen?" she asked, striding toward them. The two facing her straightened and the others turned to see what had captured their interest. She paused a few feet away and gripped the bottle in her hands.

"Well, well. What have we here?" The closest man, a round-faced fellow with pomaded hair, looked up at her with sly speculation.

"I am the owner of this establishment, sirs, and as such, your hostess." On impulse, she made a deep, sardonic curtsey. Sensing she had taken them off guard and intending to capitalize on it, she looked up…straight into a pair of golden eyes set in a strongly chiseled face.

She froze for a moment, absorbing the fact that the man's dark hair was given to waves, his skin was sun-burnished, and his broad, full lips curled languidly up on one side. As their gazes met, his half smile faded and his eyes darkened. With *interest*. His stare dragged across her skin like a match, igniting something she seldom experienced these days: anticipation.

Suppressing a shiver, she jerked her gaze away and it landed next on a tall, fleshy man with thinning hair and a distinctive V-shaped beard.

The blood drained from her head.

She knew that face.

All of Britain knew it.

Merciful Heaven. Was it possible Carson hadn't recognized their future king?

JACK ST. LAWRENCE froze with his ale cup halfway to his lips, his eyes fixed on the honey-haired beauty coiled into a deep curtsey a few inches from his outstretched legs. She was of middling height, but that was the only thing average about her. Her carriage was nothing short of regal; her abundant hair shone with fiery lights; her delicate face was clear and arresting, and—*damn*—underneath that starched blouse and fitted skirt she had curves that could make a bishop forget it was Sunday.

The pleasant ale-buzz in his head evaporated in a rush of unexpected heat. Then she looked up, and damned if she didn't have eyes as blue as a summer sky—big, luminous pools of liquid get-lost-in-me—that were returning his stare with what could only be called *interest.*

Before he could react, she jerked her head to the side and her gaze fell on Bertie. Jack watched her color drain and her eyes widen with recognition of the Prince of Wales. He'd seen that reaction before, from women of all ranks and stations. Surprise and awe, followed close on by *eagerness.*

Glancing at the rest of the prince's companions, he found them grinning, licking their lips, assessing her with lusty anticipation. Dammit. They were already half-sauced and getting rowdier by the minute. The last thing he needed was a sexual hot coal to juggle. He'd already had a close call with the little tavern maid who had brought them fresh pitchers of ale.

He had winced when they'd grabbed and fondled her, and was on the verge of intervening when the barrel-chested innkeeper appeared and roared for the girl to get back to her duties. Shocked by the innkeeper's interference, his companions had let the terrified girl scramble from the table and laughed it off as they turned back to their drinking.

He had heaved a silent sigh and downed another gulp of

the brew he'd been nursing for the better part of an hour. He didn't relish having to rein in his companions. They could be a handful. Unfortunately, they were *his* handful. When he hunted with the prince, it was his responsibility to see that things never got too far out of hand.

The heir to Britain's throne and empire, Prince Albert Edward—"Bertie" to his friends—leaned forward and looked the woman over, letting his gaze linger on her breasts before raising it to her face. He smiled, clearly pleased with what he saw. When he held out a meaty hand, she accepted it with aplomb and gave a second, rather charming dip.

"And you, good sir," she said, her lush mouth curving into a perfect cupid's bow. "Which 'Jack' would you be? Not Sprat, clearly."

*Sweet Jesus.* Had she just made reference to Bertie's girth? His companions gave low *oooh*'s that slid into muffled laughter, which caused the prince to drop her hand and resettle his vest over his bulging middle with a sharp tug…deciding whether to be a good sport about it.

Clearly in the grip of madness, the chit blundered on.

"No, no, don't tell me. Not Jack O. Lantern either—far too handsome for that. Nor Jack Ketch—too lively. Nor Jack A. Dandy—though you certainly are well-dressed enough for the part." She bit her lip and then eyed him with flirtatious appreciation. "Clearly, sir, a man of your superior aspect and august bearing could only be…*Union Jack.*"

A howl of approval went up from the others.

She produced a mischievous smile, which the prince returned.

"By damn, you're a perceptive wench, you are," he declared, grabbing her hand and using it to reel her closer.

"So I've been told, sir." She exerted just enough resistance to keep from being drawn down onto his lap. "And my 'perception' says that you and your company of gentlemen are in high spirits this evening."

A raw, male kind of laughter was their response. She was flirting with disaster. Literally. Jack straightened in his chair, tensing. If she didn't watch her step, she would find herself in serious trouble. Times five.

"I've taken the liberty of asking our innkeeper to prepare some of our special wassail for you. It's the finest for counties around." She swept the men with a playful grin. "Known far and wide to corrupt church deacons, improve the looks of spinsters and cure seven kinds of scurvy."

The prince's booming laughter brought a dazzling smile to her memorable features, tinged, perhaps, with a bit of relief.

"You say this is your inn?" the prince said, studying her. "The last time I was here, I was greeted by the owner himself. A fellow named Eller."

"Squire Eller was my husband, sir. Upon his death two years ago, the house and inn passed to me."

"You're a widow then." The prince raised an eyebrow and smiled.

Just then a large bowl of warm, spice-fragrant wassail arrived in the innkeeper's beefy arms, and the prince allowed the woman to pull away from him in order to serve it. Shortly, the sounds of a spirited fiddle wafted through the inn, growing louder as an old man appeared, warming up his strings.

*Music.* Jack studied the bold-as-brass widow with mild surprise. *To soothe the savage beasts. Very smart indeed.*

The old boy's first selection was appropriate: the lively, patriotic, "Drink Little England Dry." As the widow ladled out the wassail, she began to hum and then to sing. When she served the prince, she motioned for him to join her. He looked her over, as if deciding whether she might be worth the effort, then threw back his head and belted out the lyrics. His participation startled his companions. They glanced at each other and, as she served them, introduced themselves by their assumed names and joined in.

Soon all were singing and drinking except Jack, who scooted his chair back a few inches and watched the wily widow and his fellow hunters from beneath lowered lids. Clever she might be, but the odds were not in her favor. What was she thinking, flirting with them all?

As she handed him his cup and urged him to take up the verse, he met her eye and shook his head—hoping she would take it as the warning it was. When she merely shrugged and went on to the next man, he buried his nose in his drink and wished that for once he could just get pissing drunk himself.

For three years he'd hunted and gambled and dined with the prince…handling details and smoothing over sticky situations. He had a reputation for clear-headedness and loyalty… the legacy of his clear-headed and loyal family. Following a longstanding English tradition, they had given up a sizeable parcel of land to enlarge Bertie's grounds at Sandringham when the prince's home had been built adjacent to their family seat. The prince had rewarded that generosity by drawing the stalwart St. Lawrence sons into his circle and allowing them to seek their fortunes in his exalted company.

Jack sighed. Not that Bertie's exalted company had included any marriageable heiresses of late. The future monarch was partial to "hunting" in places populated by *his* favorite quarry: married women.

The old fiddler—Farley, the widow called him—transitioned seamlessly into another familiar tune: "Dance for Your Daddy."

"Surely, gentlemen, you know this one, too." The widow swayed her cup in time to the music. "It's played by every town musician at every country dance in England."

All Jack's companions joined in spirited song, taking turns supplying verses, one drumming accompaniment on the tabletop. Jack groaned when she planted herself before the prince with a gallant bow and held out her hand. Bertie downed the rest of his drink, rose and began to step in time with her.

Jack struggled to tamp down the tension collecting in his loins as he watched her turn gracefully and sway with seductive pleasure. She seemed to enjoy her precarious position. But then, what woman of the world didn't love being the center of wealthy, powerful men's attentions? And she clearly was that: a woman of the world. Every smile, every word and every movement proclaimed her well-practiced in the art of flirtation.

If he needed further proof, it came as Bertie's hands began to wander over her as they danced. She slyly chided him and rearranged his hands, but, Jack noted, submitted to more of the same by continuing to dance with him.

When another of the hunting party, a west-country baron seated beside him, rose to cut in, Jack grabbed his arm and pulled him back down in his chair. A second man, a marquess by title and heir to a duchy, staggered forward minutes later, intent on claiming a dance, but Jack propped his legs up on a chair in the man's path and glared him back onto his seat on a nearby bench. Each protested, but a not-so-subtle jerk of Jack's head in Bertie's direction reminded them that a woman's company was the prince's prerogative. They grumbled but reined in their irritation and settled back in spirits-soaked curiosity to watch their prince's unusual conquest.

As surely as one song led to another, one bowl of wassail led to another. The more they sang, the more deeply they imbibed, and it didn't take much of a wit to deduce that that was the cunning widow's intent. Jack felt a growing admiration for her determination and no small relief that her plan was working. If it had failed, he would have found himself up to his arse in trouble, along with her.

His companions continued to mellow, their rum-weighted eyes shining with memories as they began to recount tales of first dances and first loves. He groaned quietly. Having to listen to their sentimental ramblings while cursedly sober was almost more than he could take.

And having to watch the tempting widow settle on a stool by the prince's knees and allow him to tousle her hair and fondle her neck soon had him rigid with unwelcome heat. Especially when she looked his way with those electric-blue eyes and caught him staring at her. She gave him a provocative little smile that set the skin of his belly on fire.

Mariah finally allowed herself to relax a bit as she sat by the prince's knee. The camaraderie that developed as the rum and music worked their magic surprised her. She doubted these worldly, overprivileged men had ever had a night quite like this one. The prince had lowered his guard and begun to muss her hair affectionately, as if she were a cherished pet. She might make it through the evening without her heels in the air after all.

As the light from the hearth lowered, out came campaigning songs and sentimental favorites that made the men's faces soften further…all but the dark, handsome "Jack" who had withheld himself from the merriment and wassail, but not from searing looks in her direction. It was a relief when he slouched in his chair, laid his head back, and closed his memorable eyes.

The clock struck one and the cups were filled yet again.

"Never had s-such fun with m' trousers on," the prince said thickly, after the mantel clock struck two. Swiping a meaty hand across his drink-reddened face, he propped his drooping head on his palm. There was a weak "hear, hear" and a mute wave from a sluggish hand across the room.

Fatigue and drink claimed them one by one. Jack O. Lantern laid his head on a table; Jack A. Dandy sprawled on his back on a bench, snoring loudly, and Jack Ketch pulled a second chair over to prop his feet up and closed his eyes. Jack Sprat staggered off toward the stairs and managed to haul himself—hand over hand—up to his room.

As the prince's eyes closed and he sank irretrievably into his cups, the bronze-eyed Jack, whose alias—by process of elimination—was Jack B. Nimble, became more alert. Though he still slouched in his chair, Mariah sensed an awareness about him that belied his appearance of dozing.

When the prince's head hit the top rail of his chair, she saw Nimble Jack sit straighter. When the prince began to snore, his eyes opened fully.

Mariah waved Old Farley to a halt and gave him a grateful smile. The old fiddler nodded, rose, and shuffled off to his quarters in the stables…leaving her and Nimble Jack the only ones awake in the public room.

Her heart started to pound as he rose from his chair. He was taller than she'd realized, and his broad shoulders and long, muscular legs gave him an aura of physical strength that made her want to step back. She didn't, but regretted it when he loomed over her and her knees weakened.

When he spoke, his deep tones generated a shocking vibration in her skin. She had to shake herself mentally to make sense of what he'd said.

"—cannot leave him here." He took the unconscious prince by the arms, pulling him forward in the chair. "Show me the way to his room and help me get him into bed."

She fought the urge to rub the gooseflesh his voice raised

on her arms and shoulders. What was the matter with her? She hadn't had that much of Carson's brain-fuddling brew.

She stepped up onto a chair to grab a lantern from the rafter while Jack tried unsuccessfully to hoist the limp royal onto his shoulders. With a huff, she inserted herself under one of the prince's arms, dragging it up and around her shoulders. Muttering irritably, Jack took the other arm and helped her haul the bulky future monarch to his feet.

"Come on, Bertie, give us some help here," he growled.

But it was only when she spoke—"Come, Your Highness, time for bed. You do want to go to *bed,* don't you?"—that some sense of what was happening penetrated the fog in the prince's head. He roused enough to bear some of his own weight and allow them to propel him forward.

Together—banging and bumping, trading orders and cautions—they dragged the prince up the stairs to the inn's finest guest room. On the way through the door, his knees buckled. She dropped the lantern to use both hands to help hold him up. They half carried, half dragged him to the bed and dumped him on it.

They stood side by side staring at their future king, breathing hard.

"Should we remove his boots?" she whispered, starkly aware of Nimble Jack's broad chest rising and falling and of the mélange of intriguing male scents about him. The only light available was from the lantern she had dropped just inside the door. Its glow reflected off the plank floor, casting the upper half of the room in soft shadows. When she looked up, he was staring at her. Tall, dark and potent.

Heaven help her, she stared back…at least enough to see that the bronze disks of his eyes had warmed with a rising heat…that his lips were parted…that his shoulders seemed to grow with each ragged exhalation. She couldn't get her breath.

The next thing she knew he was moving toward her. She stepped back. His stride lengthened and suddenly his body met hers and swept her back against the wall beside the door. The impact set a pitcher and basin on the nearby washstand rattling.

She was stunned by both the physical contact and her own lack of resistance to it. Then slowly, so slowly that she could have easily escaped, he raised both of his hands, palms out, and planted them against the wall on either side of her. There he paused, waiting, looking at her.

She lifted her face enough to search at close range the features she had somehow memorized over the course of the evening. Those eyes—molten pools of gold…that skin—sleek and drawn taut over strongly carved cheekbones…those lips—broad and neatly bordered, just inches from hers. He roused something in her, something dormant, something not altogether welcome.

She didn't mean to do it, made no decision, formed no conscious intent. The impulse came from memories stored in her very bones and sinews that made her stretch and arch her body upward, against his.

With a sound that was half groan, half growl, he leaned in and pressed her back against the wall. His body was hot and hard but strangely not shocking against hers; the intimacy was no longer foreign. She *remembered*. With every breath his body moved against hers like a tide lapping, testing, caressing the shore. Her skin came alive beneath her clothes. More, she wanted more contact. She wanted to *feel* him.

Her desire to touch and be touched rattled her to her very core. Trembling, she shoved her hands out to the sides… palms pressed flat against the wall…below his. And suddenly she understood why his hands were there.

When she opened her eyes and looked up, her gaze fastened on his parted lips. Kisses, she remembered kisses… mouth to mouth…intimate silk and moist heat. Her lips felt hot and sensitive, expectant. She wetted them, and gasped silently when she *tasted* the sweetness from the rum on his breath. She swept her tongue across her lip, luring him closer…so close that she could feel his warmth radiating into her skin and his breath curling across her cheek. But his head dropped to the side, and his mouth skimmed her temple, her ear, the side of her throat. The sensations were so tentative—was he touching her or was that his breath against her skin?

Cascading sensations sent a hum through her blood and a shiver through her body. Her nipples drew taut and tingled in a way she hadn't experienced in a very long time. Holding her breath, she pressed her breasts into him, dragging them along his ribs. He countered her motion, giving her the stimulation she sought and adding a small, tantalizing undulation of his own…one that confirmed the effect she had on him.

Heat rushed to her breasts and her sex, concentrating and intensifying the sensations so that her sensitive flesh burned with the desire for contact. When his knee probed her skirt, she instinctively let it slide between her own and gradually, savoring the yielding, parted her thighs. Steam billowed through her senses as he fitted himself against her. Breath snagged in her throat as sensation mounted like waves.

More, she wanted more.

She pulled her hands from the wall, seized his face between them, and pressed her lips to his. He went perfectly still, and something in her clicked like the switch of an electric light. She froze as reality fanned away some of the steam in her senses.

Abruptly, he peeled himself from her body, leaving her to stagger slightly as she sank back against the wall. The chilled air that invaded the space between them was a rude shock. She was trembling and felt as if her knees had turned to rubber.

Sweet Heaven. What had happened to her?

Her mind clutched at impressions: his burning stare and his hands clenched at his sides…the throb in her woman's flesh…the prince's vigorous snores…the open door only three feet away…

She escaped into the hall and down the steps—having to hang on to the railing to remain upright. She headed through the inn's darkened kitchen and pulled her cloak from the rack by the door as Carson rose from his chair by the hearth. His son, half awake and protesting being dislodged from his father's lap, clung to his leg.

"You all right, Miz Eller?" The innkeeper dragged his hands over his face, glancing toward the dim glow from the public room.

"They're out—the lot of them."

"Just like you planned, eh?" The innkeeper flashed a weary grin.

"Just li-ike—" her voice cracked "—I planned."

"Want me to walk ye up to th' house, miz?"

"No—thank you," she said, grateful for the darkness that hid her burning face. "Morning will come too early for you as it is." She settled the cloak around her shoulders and pulled up its hood. "And it wasn't *me* that drank a hogshead of rum this night."

"No, it weren't." Carson chuckled. "Ye were somethin,' miz."

"Yes. Well." She paused with her hand on the door latch, before stepping out into the chilled autumn night. "I think we'd both be advised to forget everything that happened here tonight."

# 2

MARIAH stewed with dread the next day, even after giving orders to turn away all callers with word that she was indisposed. So when Carson's boy arrived in the afternoon with word that the prince had received a message that put him in a bad humor, climbed aboard his horse and ridden off to Scotland, she wilted with relief.

She had been delivered from the consequences of her brazen behavior.

She should have felt grateful, but instead she was seized by an unholy restlessness. Stalking down to the inn, she went from room to room, sorting and rearranging, clearing rooms and then moving the furniture back. Nothing pleased her. If she hadn't feared a servant revolt, she'd have begun scrubbing walls and pounding rugs, spring-cleaning six months early.

At wits' end, she sent for Old Farley to bring some soothing music up to the house. But she sent the old boy away again shortly after he began to play. Every note evoked the memory of a brooding golden-eyed presence.

Even a week later, the restlessness had not lessened.

Desperate to spend the tension inside her, she put on her oldest clothes and went to work in her garden one morning. The oak trees were bare, the flowers had died back, and the shrubbery—all but the balsam and holly—had surrendered to the cold and shortened days. But even here, on her knees in her beloved garden, she had trouble banishing thoughts of that night.

"Tart," she said irritably, jamming her spade into the cold, dark earth. The autumn sun was too pale and remote to warm the ground where she was planting bulbs beside the arbor walk. Her gloves were caked with wet soil, her fingers were half frozen, and her back ached from the bending. But she was determined to set these blessed daffodils.

"That's how you are behaving, you know. Like a *tart*." She straightened onto her protesting knees. "I am *not*."

Glowering, she stabbed the earth again and snatched up another handful of papery golden bulbs.

"I did nothing wrong. *He* accosted *me*."

Though to be fair, *accosted* was painting it a bit black. He hadn't kissed her. Hadn't set hands on her. There wasn't even a name for what he'd done to her. But it was intimate and pleasurable and furtive, which, by all decent lights, made it wrong, wrong, wrong.

And just like that, she was immersed in the memory she had tried to keep at bay and reliving those erotic sensations in the prince's darkened sleeping room. Warmth and breath commingled…bodies pressed hard together, hungry, straining for more… Her throat tightened at the thought and her breath came quicker. It was the strange nature of the encounter, she told herself, that made it so difficult to dismiss.

Curse "Jack B. Nimble" for rousing such desires in her.

After Mason had died she had locked away that part of her. It hadn't been easy; her worldly older husband had been a remarkable lover who tutored her expertly and boldly cultivated her passions. When he died unexpectedly, she had been blooming into her sexual prime and struggled nightly to subdue the desires he had so deftly roused. But then she learned of the entailment that placed her husband's land in the hands of distant relatives. Left with no income, only an aging house and a coaching inn in bad repair, she had to scramble to survive and poured the energy of her stubborn desires into the hard work of remaking the inn into an establishment capable of supporting herself and her people.

The result was that the Eller-Stapleton had never looked so fine or received such brisk trade. It seemed, after two grueling years, that her life and her business were on the brink of flourishing—despite the debts she had incurred—and that was satisfaction enough.

Until a week ago.

She shoved bulb after bulb into the damp, pungent earth, each time giving the dirt above it a smack, daring the bulb to show its head until spring.

Thus occupied, she didn't hear Carson's boy approach.

"Miz?" She turned so sharply that she fell back on her rear, scattering the bulbs she held across the ground. Young Jamie stood with hands in his pockets and a grin on his round, cold-reddened face. "Ye got callers, miz."

She pressed a hand to her chest to contain the racing of her heart.

"Yes? Who is it?" The cold had set her nose running. She sniffed.

"Gen'lmen. Pa said I should bring 'em up." He stepped to the side and revealed two men standing on the path some distance away.

Mariah scowled at their caped greatcoats and black top hats. Whoever they were, they dressed like bankers. The thought made her heart seize.

She started to rise and realized her skirts were twisted around her, exposing her old woolen stockings and muddy boots. She knew there was dried dirt on her face, where she'd pushed her hair back earlier; she looked a mess. But then, she hadn't invited them here. Clumsy from the cold, she staggered to her feet and brushed her skirts before realizing that her dirt-caked gloves were making her even more of a mess. Scowling, she pulled them off and threw them into the wooden trug that held her tools.

The men's backs were to her; they seemed to be surveying her garden.

"You wished to see me, gentlemen?"

They turned as she approached.

She stopped dead on the path as her gaze connected with a pair of cool bronze-colored eyes and the bottom dropped out of her stomach.

*Him.*

"EDGAR MARCHANT, madam—*Baron* Marchant," the shorter man introduced himself, tipping his hat. It took her a moment to recognize "Jack O. Lantern"…the prince's friend with the round face and pomaded hair.

"John St. Lawrence, Mrs. Eller." Jack B. Nimble removed his hat, and her knees weakened. Broad shoulders, dark hair, golden eyes; he was exactly as she had remembered him.

She crossed her arms and refused to give in to the panic blooming in her chest.

"Gentlemen," she said, thinking that despite their smooth manners and expensive clothes, they were anything but.

JACK ST. LAWRENCE took in Mariah Eller's dirt-streaked clothes and rosy, dirt-smudged cheeks. This was hardly how he expected to be received by the feisty widow. She looked like a servant girl sent out to weed the kitchen herb patch. Younger and fresher than he had recalled, and even more appealing. It was a good thing Marchant had spoken first; his own throat had tightened.

"We have come on an errand of some importance," Marchant intoned with lordly precision. "Perhaps you would like us to return in an hour or two, so that you might have time to—" he glanced at her clothing "—prepare to receive our news."

It was the wrong thing to say, apparently. She seemed startled by Marchant's offer of time to make herself presentable, then offended by it. Her gaze darted to the basket by her feet; she looked as if she could gladly drive a garden tool through the baron's heart.

*Damn and blast Bertie,* Jack thought, sending him on such an errand. He was used to handling matters and seeing to it that the prince's desires were carried out. Capable and always in control, he was the perfect man for a sensitive mission. But not *this* mission.

He dreaded facing this woman the way he dreaded a dentist with a pair of pliers. And he didn't want to think about why.

"Anything you have to say to me, sir, you may say here and now. As you can see—" she gestured to her bulbs and tools "—I am quite busy. I doubt there will be many more days this season suitable for planting."

A very bad feeling developed in the pit of Jack's stomach as her chin came up. It was *his* presence that raised her hackles, he was sure of it.

"At the very least, let us be seated." Marchant gestured to a nearby pair of stone benches in a leafless bower among the hedges. After a moment she exhaled irritably and complied with the request.

Feeling stiff all over, fearing his knees might not bend, Jack waved Marchant to the seat on the bench beside her while he stood nearby.

"We bring sincerest greetings from the Prince of Wales," Marchant declared with a smile. "No doubt you recognized him during his recent stay at your fine inn."

"Of course," she said, obviously still nettled.

"He has asked us to convey to you how impressed he was with your hospitality, your ingenuity and the warmth of your person," the baron continued. "He was quite taken with you, Mrs. Eller. And he has entrusted to us a somewhat delicate—"

"Are you going to sit, Mr. St. Lawrence?" She pinned Jack with a look, her tone peppery.

God, they were making a hash of it, he thought.

"Certainly." He sat down on the opposite bench, as far from her as he could get and still have stone beneath his bum cheeks. "As the baron has said, the prince was quite taken with you. It is rare, I can tell you, for His Highness to be so…so…"

He found himself staring into big blue eyes filled with questions and suspicions and not a little indignation. He struggled to recall the persuasions he'd practiced in his mind on the way down from Scotland.

"…so relaxed in the presence of a lady…um…"

"A lady with whom he has not established *relations*," the baron supplied smoothly. "To come to the point, Mrs. Eller, the prince wishes to see you again." He studied the puzzlement in her face and came right out with it. "He wishes to establish personal relations with you, Mrs. Eller. Very *close*…personal…relations. St. Lawrence and I are here to make the necessary arrangements."

She blinked and looked from the baron to Jack.

"Relations? He wishes to have close…oh…oh, my Lord…*relations* with me?" Her shock was too artless not to be genuine.

Jack had the urge to knock the smirk from Marchant's face. In the seconds it took him to master that shocking impulse, she shot to her feet.

"That is absurd. What would the prince want with a simple widow who—" She stiffened, reddening. "Take your ugly little joke back to your friends and tell them that their insult found its mark and was keenly felt."

"Mrs. Eller!" The baron was on his feet before her, alarmed now. "This is no jest, I assure you. We have come at the behest of the Prince of Wales himself." From the breast pocket of his coat he produced a letter as evidence. "If you doubt the authenticity of our mission, let the prince himself reassure you. You must surely see that this is not a matter he is free to undertake on his own behalf. He has entrusted both his desire and his honor to us in this matter. I assure you, we are faithful to that trust."

She stood for a moment, regarding the letter as if it were a snake. Then with a fierce look at Jack, she took it from the baron and inspected the royal seal before breaking it open. The trembling of the paper was the only sign that what was penned on the vellum made any impact on her.

"I believe, gentlemen," she said, sounding as if her mouth were dry, "that the events of a week ago may have given His Highness a mistaken notion of my character."

The baron's eyes narrowed and his oily smile appeared.

"I believe the prince knows precisely what conclusions to draw about a woman who drinks men under her table, flaunts her availability before half a dozen men at a time, and then hauls the heir to the throne into bed with her." He tilted his head to look down his nose. "The prince has already *tasted* the nature of your character, madam. And you are fortunate indeed that he has found the flavor to his liking."

"Tasted my…but…the prince…" She looked to Jack in disbelief.

He scowled pointedly at her, then looked away…hoping she would see what had to be seen…that he hadn't disabused the prince of the idea that something had happened between him and the widow.

"This is a surprise for you, clearly," Jack said emphatically to mask his discomfort. "But I would counsel that you think well before rejecting such an opportunity. The prince's fancy does not usually dwell for long in one place…and yet the honor and the benefit to you may be such that you will be well-fixed for life. The prince is very generous to his friends."

"So he is, our beloved prince," the baron added. "Most generous."

"An honor?" she said. "To serve as a paramour to a married man?"

"To our future monarch," the baron corrected. "Make no mistake, madam. Ladies who serve the prince in such a personal capacity are not regarded as mere courtesans or 'paramours.' These ladies, great and small, serve both crown and country and are regarded with utmost respect."

Her hand tightened visibly on the letter. She seemed to have difficulty getting her breath.

Jack scowled. She must surely understand that she had been selected for a singular honor, one that dukes of the realm actively encouraged their lady wives to seek, knowing that with *fancy* came *favor*. However, she had not been bred to the class that sought advancement above all else. The turmoil in her was disconcerting. If she truly had some moral objection—

He caught himself. Not hardly. She was hot enough for a man's touch—even a man she had hardly met. His ears heated at the thought of how he knew that. And she was a *widow*, after all. It wasn't as if she had vows to observe or a maiden-head to hoard. If she had a brain in her head she would come around quickly and take Bertie's offer.

"Perhaps you need time to think it through," Jack said. "To see the advantage to all sides in this arrangement."

"Of course." The baron leaned closer. "And while you are thinking, madam, be sure to consider the sizeable debts you have incurred on behalf of your quaint establishment. One word from the prince and your thousand-pound loan can be paid and stricken from both ledger and memory. A different word, however, could bring the note due this very day. You are surely clever enough to see the advantage in allying yourself to such power."

"I believe she has the idea," Jack said, stepping back and pulling the baron out of her way. "Shall we call for your answer, say, at four-thirty?"

Rigid with control, she picked up her garden tools, set them in a nearby wheelbarrow, then stalked off down the path to the house. The *shush* of pea gravel under her feet sounded uncannily like the swish of silk petticoats. Jack felt a curious clutch in his chest at the thought.

When she disappeared into the house, he came to his senses and found Marchant wearing a smug expression.

"What are you smiling about?" he asked the wily baron.

"She's a hot one, all right." The baron thumped his arm. "But I can't say I envy Bertie the trouble she'll be."

"*If* she agrees." He stuck his hat on his head and struck off down the path to the inn.

"Oh, she'll agree," the baron said with a wicked chuckle, falling in beside him. "Her eyes lit like Fawkes' Night bonfires when I said the word *debts*. Take a lesson, Jack my boy. Money trumps morality every time."

# 3

"I WANT a fire, a brandy and a bath," Mariah declared as she burst into the kitchen and ripped off her jacket, muffler and rubber boots. *"Now."*

The household staff—cook, butler, housemaid and kitchen boy—stared in confusion at her and then at each other. Brandy? At noon?

Robert, her stoop-shouldered butler, who more closely resembled a question mark with each passing year, shuffled off mumbling and squinting as he thrust his keys to arm's length to fish for the one that opened the liquor cabinet. Her rotund maid-of-all-work, Mercy, trudged up the stairs to light the boiler in the bathing room, pausing to rub her back along the way so that her mistress would see how the extra work aggravated her lumbago. Aggie, her ancient cook, stood gaping as Mariah ordered afternoon tea for three and instructed her to send to the butcher for a prime cut of braising beef.

"I'm of a mind to sink my teeth into some red meat tonight," Mariah declared, seizing her brandy and stomping up the stairs.

Old Robert and even older Aggie exchanged looks. They hadn't been asked to serve red meat at Eller House since the old master had died. That combined with spirits-drinking and bath-taking in the middle of the week—*the middle of the day!*—confirmed that something unusual was happening.

It was almost as if the old master, Squire Eller, was back. The aged retainers shook their heads with wistful smiles. Those were the days. Old Mason had a streak in him, he did. Demanded his fun. Accompanied by a sizeable belt of brandy before and a hunk of juicy beefsteak after.

So, who or what had roused their mistress into such a state?

Mariah had no thought to spare for servant curiosity. Her heart was pounding and her limbs were icy by the time she reached her bedroom. Dread crawled up her spine the way it must in an animal caught in a trap and awaiting its fate. She was indeed "caught," and the fact that the trap was partly of her own making made it that much worse.

To protect her property, she'd flaunted herself before a group of idle, arrogant noblemen, never guessing that the true price of one night's peace would prove steeper still. Now she had to pay with that unique currency that women had used to acquire safety and security since the beginning of time.

The men's words came around again and again in her head as she paced her room, waiting for Mercy to draw her bath. *Very close personal relations… Quite taken with her…* Having "tasted" her, the prince had found her "flavor" to his liking.

That was what outraged her most, she realized. John St. Lawrence had "nimbly" failed to inform their future king that the royal member had been limp and unresponsive—incapable of manly service—when they helped him to his bed. Why hadn't the wretch told the prince the truth? Then she recalled the warning on St. Lawrence's face when she'd started to correct the notion that the prince had bedded her, and she guessed why.

The royal pride. His companions were pledged to it as a matter of patriotic service. And if honoring it meant allowing the prince to think he'd bedded a woman when he hadn't…to them it was a small price to pay. Of course they'd feel that way, she thought with a moan. It wasn't *their* lives being disrupted, *their* honor being claimed or *their* bodies being bartered.

Damned *men*.

She was wise enough in the ways of the world, however, to see that if she turned down this "generous offer" she would be inviting trouble that might only begin with debts being called in early. Clearly, they had made inquiries to learn her circumstances and figured out how pressure could be brought to bear on her. Even if the prince himself were not vindictive, the men around him would never allow such an insult to the royal pride to go unredressed.

A ROYAL MISTRESS. As she descended the stairs that afternoon, toward the interview that would change her life, she paused to give herself a final check in the ornate hall mirror. The woman staring back at her didn't look especially wicked or licentious. It occurred to her to wonder what a future king looked for in a mistress. What if the prince actually did bed her and she proved not to be to his tastes after all?

She smoothed the elongated bodice of her best blue challis dress, puffed her leg-o'-mutton sleeves, and checked the mother-of-pearl buttons at her wrists. Her green dress might have highlighted her hair better, but the blue brought out her eyes.

Not, she scolded herself, that she wanted "Jack B. Nimble" to notice her eyes. She just wanted him and his arrogant comrade to see that she was a woman of stature, not to be trifled with or condescended to. The bastards.

Chiding herself for her language, she ran a hand over her upswept hair, brushed at the dusting of simple powder on her reddened cheeks, and straightened her collar and cameo... avoiding her own eyes in the mirror.

In the spacious front parlor, Old Robert was shuffling in from the dining room with a rattling tray of cups, saucers and spoons. Older Aggie labored along behind him with a fresh cloth for the tea table and a tiered plate caddie filled with tea cakes and sandwiches. The pair looked downright frazzled. She sighed. She needed some younger servants.

The hearth-lighting and table-draping continued until Old Robert was called away to answer the front door. He returned shortly with the baron and St. Lawrence in tow. A motion toward her head reminded the old butler of his duty. He grabbed the hats from the men's hands and yanked the coats from their shoulders…doddering out with the garments dragging on the floor behind him.

Mariah stood near the venerable marble hearth, glad of the heat at her back, feeling every muscle in her body tense as "Nimble Jack" St. Lawrence crossed her parlor with an easy, athletic stride. She extended a hand to the baron and then to *him,* knowing it was the civil thing to do and dreading it all the same.

As Nimble Jack bowed—"Mrs. Eller"—she caught the scents of sandalwood and warmed wool and felt a flash of the memory she'd tried to bury in her garden that morning. His dark hair looked soft, his shoulders were broad, and his hand around hers was warm and firm, like the rest of—

"Baron. Mr. St. Lawrence." She braced herself and gestured to the linen-draped table. "I thought perhaps we would have tea as we talk."

An unctuous smile spread over the baron's face and he glanced at St. Lawrence. They read in her reception the answer they hoped to receive.

"Excellent. The prince will be quite pleased," the baron said, glowing at this positive outcome. "I imagine you have questions for us."

And just like that, it was done. She was to become a mistress to the Prince of Wales. She glanced at St. Lawrence as the baron held her chair for her at the tea table. The baron was ebullient, but "Nimble Jack" seemed oddly contained upon learning of his mission's success.

She rang the china bell on the table to summon the tea.

"I suppose my first question is, will I have to remove to London?"

"I should imagine that will depend on a number of things," the baron said, relishing his role. "His Highness travels a great deal. His secretary makes the necessary arrangements. I would never presume to speak for the prince in matters unauthorized, but I gathered that he intends to join you here in the Lake Country. He is fond of country air and hunting." A weasel-like smile appeared. "But, of course, there will be your husband to consider."

She frowned, wondering if he had taken leave of his senses. "My husband, sir, is deceased."

"Of course he is." The baron gave a tense little laugh and she saw St. Lawrence stiffen. "I meant to say your *new* husband."

Just then Old Robert rushed in with a silver teapot that he had forgotten to pick up with a mitt. The old fellow dropped it onto the table with a sloshing thud—"Tea be sarved"—and then tottered out, grumbling as he nursed his overheated hand.

"My what?" She turned to the baron, her blood stopped in her veins.

"Your new husband, madam." The baron straightened, pulling authority around him like a cloak. "The prince would never enter into relations with an unmarried woman. That would never do. To leave a woman he is associated with unprotected and exposed to the world…the prince would never be so callous."

Her jaw loosened but thankfully did not drop.

"I am a widow, sir," she said, leaning forward. "I live independently and have no husband to object to such an arrangement. How can the prince possibly imagine I would wish to acquire one now?"

"But you *must* acquire one, madam, or relations with the prince cannot proceed." The baron looked scandalized by the prospect. "The prince has made it his firm—and most wise—practice to spend time only with ladies whose husbands can provide comfort for them once his time with them is done." The baron produced a handkerchief and dabbed his moist lip.

"This is absurd," she said, looking at St. Lawrence, who took up the argument.

"If I may be blunt." He clenched his jaw, looking as if he'd just sucked a lemon. "There is always the possibility of *consequences* from such relations. The prince has left no 'consequences' in his path to date, and is determined to see that any born to his special friends will have fathers of their own. As heir to our good queen's throne and the future head of the Church of England, to do otherwise would be unthinkable to him."

Mariah felt the flush of color she had just experienced now drain from her face. *Consequences:* a polite way of saying *children.* The prince intended to leave no royal bastards in his wake. Fastidious of him, she thought furiously, to take his future roles as seriously as he took his pleasures. He bedded women thither and yon but insisted, whether from fear of public opinion or his own moral quirk, that the natural *consequences* of those liaisons never be laid at his doorstep.

"Why on earth would I wish to exchange vows with a man, only to betray them with the prince?" she demanded, gripping the edge of the table.

"Because," St. Lawrence said tightly, "it is necessary. And if you are anything, Mrs. Eller, you are a woman who recognizes the necessary and turns it to her advantage."

She felt struck physically by that assessment. Rising abruptly from the table, she went to the long windows that overlooked the side yard. Anger roiled in her as she gripped the sash. So that was what they thought of her. Clever. Contriving. Conveniently amoral.

The full weight of the situation bore down on her. She was a woman whose behavior had left room for assumption. A woman with no man to "protect" her. A woman who could be acquired, used and discarded like a pair of outmoded trousers. Her insignificant life could be turned upside-down without a second thought should she fail to cooperate. To accept such conditions would mean that *she* would be the one to pay for the prince's pleasures…*with a lifetime of marital servitude.*

All because the prince fancied her.

Eyes burning, she turned to look at them. The baron sat with his arms crossed and St. Lawrence toyed with a teacup from the tray. Neither seemed at all chagrined by the demands they placed on her.

Then it occurred to her in a stroke: if she couldn't find a husband, the prince might be forced to call off the notion of bedding her.

"I fear, gentlemen, we are at an impasse. I know of no man willing to marry me and then loan me out for a spell to the Prince of Wales."

"I expect that is true." The baron's composure bordered on the smug. "We, on the other hand, know quite a few."

She was stunned. In the silence that followed, she realized that there was still more to come. With each new requirement they had slowly painted her into a corner.

"As we have said, the prince is generous," the baron continued. "There are numerous men of his acquaintance who would be willing to do him just such a favor."

"And what sort of men would they be? Barking madmen? Wastrels? Misers who would sell their grandmothers for a profit?"

"I assure you, madam—" the baron rose, looking as sincere as a weasel can look "—the men on St. Lawrence's list are gentlemen, one and all."

She looked to Nimble Jack, who pulled an envelope from his inner breast pocket and laid it on the tea table beside her china cups. The cad! He had arrived that morning with a list of agreeable cuckolds in his pocket!

"You came prepared," she said, struggling with rising outrage.

"The prince surrounds himself with resourceful men," Jack said.

"Resourceful," she echoed. So that was how the wretch saw himself.

She turned back to the window and clamped her arms around her waist. The prince had a whole kingdom of "resourceful" men to see to his welfare. She, on the other hand, had no one. No parents, no brothers or sisters, no uncles or aunts to intervene on her behalf. That was how she had fallen into the squire's hands in the first place. The magistrate overseeing the sale of her deceased father's property had insisted that, as a girl alone, marriage was her only option. And as it happened, his friend Squire Eller was in need of a wife. In the end, she was just one more asset the judge dispersed to a man whose good will would ease his own way in life.

But she was not that naive little seventeen-year-old girl anymore. She had learned the ways of the world and the men who ran it. The years of hard work since her husband died had stunted her reactions, dulled her responses. But no longer. Resourceful? She'd show the wretches *resourceful*.

She'd find a way to get out of this intolerable fix or die trying!

"No matter what you think of me, gentlemen, the prince's proposal is shocking to a woman of my background and experience. Make no mistake, I would not consider accepting the overtures of a married man, even those from His Highness the Prince of Wales, if I had a gracious way of declining them.

"I must, however, demand a choice in those small matters which are of interest to no one but myself. The prince may be my friend and supporter for a few months or even a year or two, but I will remain wedded to this 'husband' for the rest of my days. Therefore, I insist upon the right to choose the man I will marry." She pointed to the envelope. "I cannot continue unless I am assured that I may reject those men with impunity."

The baron looked anxiously to St. Lawrence, who frowned at this new wrinkle and studied her openly.

"And if you refuse all of the men on this list, what then?" he asked.

"We must have some assurance," the baron said, mopping his lip again, "that you will show good faith in seeking a husband elsewhere."

"I give you my word, sir, that I will. If that is not enough, then you must return to the prince and explain to him your predicament—that you do not believe the woman *he* selected as a mistress is worthy of *your* trust."

There was an awkward silence as they grappled with her demand.

"A time limit, then," the baron said, proposing a compromise. "Say, a fortnight. You must pledge to find and accept a husband within a fortnight."

She looked from one man to the other, turning it over in her mind.

"I think two weeks should be sufficient."

"Excellent." The baron's smile was full of relief as he rose and reached for her hand. "I'll be off, then, to deliver the good news to the prince. St. Lawrence here will see to the details. He has access to funds and the special license and will ensure that you have whatever clothing and incidentals you desire." There was a hint of challenge in his tone. "He will see to it that you are wedded within the agreed-upon time."

# 4

JACK WATCHED with an unsettled expression masking pure inner turmoil as the baron took his leave.

Damn and blast Marchant, saddling him with marrying off Mariah Eller! He had agreed to compile a list of suggested men for her to marry when it became clear that the prince was determined to go through with this idiocy, but he had never imagined it would come to this.

She'd already declared her opposition to the whole notion. What in hell made Marchant think she would actually do the deed? When he looked back at Mariah, she was settling at the table and reaching for the teapot. He sat down opposite her, gripping his knees under the tablecloth.

After pouring in silence and serving him, she reached for the envelope on the table and opened it to peruse the names inside with a frown.

"So, you're to be both minder and matchmaker." She didn't look up.

"And you're to be cooperative." He sipped his tea, wishing to hell it was Scotch whiskey.

"I intend to be, Mr. St. Lawrence. I must say, that name sounds wrong to me. I feel I should call you Jack."

His smile faded, then returned as if force-marched back.

"You may call me that if you wish, Mrs. Eller. Most do. In truth, I was the one true 'Jack' in the room that night."

"You could have saved me a great deal of grief if you had been *truer* still." She sipped her own tea with an accusing expression.

Those damnable blue eyes. *Don't look,* he told himself.

"Men loyal to the future king—" he began, focusing purposefully on the wheezing hearth.

"Refuse to tell him the truth?" she inserted. "His reign won't be one for the history books if *that* is the kind of counsel he depends upon."

He straightened and met that gaze full-on.

"You were in the room and clearly willing. What does it matter that your kiss found lips other than his?"

For a brief moment he thought he saw actual flame in the dark centers of her eyes.

"Yes, of course," she said with a razor edge. "A woman who will kiss one man will surely not scruple about kissing another. And a woman who enters a man's sleeping room will surely bed any man she finds there. For men are all the same in the dark, are they not?"

He scowled at her twist on the well-known saw: *Jane is the same as milady in the dark.* She meant to torture him with verbal thumbscrews. Lord, how he hated clever women.

"I did not mean to imply that you have no discrimination, Mrs. Eller. I merely pointed out that it could as easily have been the prince you kissed."

"No, it could not," she said, her cheeks pinker. "It may shock you to hear, sir, but I actually have standards. And bedding married men destined to rule my country is definitely outside them." She reached for the list of potential husbands and scowled at it. "With such an attitude, I am surprised that you bothered to include so many names." She set the paper down and picked up her cup, giving him an arch look.

"I wonder…what was your criteria for selection? What

about these men made you think any of them would be suitable as a husband for me?"

He expelled a quiet breath, feeling her gaze roaming him as his had just wandered her. An unwelcome heaviness was settling in his loins.

"All are unmarried and have an income of two thousand or better."

"And?" she prompted.

"And all would be willing to marry a comely young widow if it would win for them the future king's favor."

"So, I marry one of these men and serve both the prince's and this husband's carnal demands?" She seemed genuinely taken aback. "If so, I am going to be one very well-buttered bun."

He was jarred by her blunt language. "I believe it is understood that the marriage will be in name only until the prince foregoes his relationship with you. Your husband will be free to enjoy his marital rights at that time."

"Oh. Well. How fortunate for him. I am on loan to the prince for as long as he wants me to pleasure him, after which I am given back to my legal lord and master to serve his pleasures." She leaned forward, searching his face. "Forgive me, *Jack,* but I'm having trouble figuring out just what *I* get out of all this pleasuring."

*Pleasuring.* The way she said the word sent a tongue of heat licking up the inside of his belly. A phantom vignette of burying his face in her hair and sliding his hands over her warm breasts flashed through his senses.

"I believe you know very well what you will get, madam. Income…gifts…connections…" Running out of benefits, he grabbed a tea sandwich and stuffed it whole into his mouth.

A foul, vinegary taste filled his head, and he feared he might be sick. It must have shown, for she handed him the baron's unused napkin.

"Aggie's tripe 'n' turnip sandwich—not her best work," she said as he disposed of the bite and rinsed his mouth with tea. She offered him a jam tart. "This usually kills the taste."

"Good Lord." His eyes still watered as he stuffed the entire tart in his mouth and felt the beastly taste subside. "She'll poison somebody."

"She's better with more ordinary fare. She doesn't get a chance to produce her specialties often." Her smile was nothing short of taunting.

"Then you will have to make changes to your staff and upgrade your cellar. You will be expected to provide food and drink for the prince and the occasional dinner for some of his intimates."

"Oh? And will those 'intimates' include you?" she asked, freshening his cup.

"I doubt it," he said, downing more of the brew and vowing never to set foot in her presence again once this business was finished.

"You are not considered one of his 'intimates'?"

"I am pleased to say that he counts me a loyal friend. We hunt together. My family's land borders the prince's at Sandringham, and for years the prince has taken birds from our fields and dined at our table. While I am in London, I generally attend social functions with him. But as for being an 'intimate'—"

"I should think that negotiating for a mistress would certainly qualify you as one," she said with excessive sweetness. "How fortunate for him to have an 'acquaintance' willing to see him to his bed when he can no longer find it and kiss women for him when he can no longer muster a pucker."

He swallowed repeatedly—the damned tart was stuck in his throat—and then drained his cup.

"The men who hunt with the prince are charged with his

welfare, madam, and do not take their ease before seeing to his safety." He smacked the cup back onto the saucer. "And since you raised the topic, *I* kissed no one. I believe it was *you* who did the kissing."

She regarded him fiercely for a moment, probably deciding whether to unleash a bit of temper, then to his surprise gave a reasonable nod.

"So it was." The smile that bloomed from her thoughts sent a cool trickle of anxiety up his spine. "And look where it's brought me. I shall have to be much more careful about whom I kiss in the future."

He rose and went to the window to find cooler air. Every time she said the word *kiss,* his damned collar seemed to grow a bit tighter.

"It hardly seems fair that one of these men—" she joined him there, brandishing his list "—will receive such benefit without so much as raising a finger." She glanced from him to the names, and back. "Tell me, which man do you think would suit me best?"

"I have not the temerity to suggest, madam." He clasped his hands firmly behind his back and stared past her out the window.

"But you *have* had the temerity to suggest, sir. You put four men on this list, so you must have some opinion on their suitability." She motioned with the paper, inadvertently brushing his vest with it. His abdominal muscles snapped taut. "This Thomas Bickering, is he a tall man?"

"I couldn't say, madam." He refused to look at her.

"Do you know if he is portly or balding or has snuff-yellowed teeth?"

"I do not. I am not personally acquainted with the fellow."

"Yet you would marry me off to him without a blink. What about the others? Richard Stephens, Winston Martindale and Gordon Clapford?"

"Clapford lives near Grantham, but is heir to a barony somewhere in Ireland," he rattled off. "Stephens's income is from some cotton mills south of London. Martindale is a friend of the Earl of Chester's son…comes recommended by the earl. Bickering is a solicitor in Lincoln. That and the men's income is all I know about them."

Silence fell as she looked between him and the paper in her hand.

"You honestly expect me to choose one of these men to share my bed and partner my life, but you cannot tell me which is tallest, which dribbles gravy on his shirtfronts and which is stingy with his household allowance…all matters critical to the success of a marriage?"

"How on earth is a man's height significant to wedded success?"

"It is easy to see you have never been married, sir." He glanced down to find her eyes lit with feminine superiority. "Otherwise you would know how a man's *dimensions* enter into his wife's contentment. How can I be expected to choose without seeing, much less experiencing these men?"

She leaned against the windowsill, her eyes darting over some private vision, running her hands up her arms. Nice hands. Long-fingered and graceful. Probably strong enough to—damn it!

What was he thinking, giving her more than one name at a time? Women took weeks to make up their minds about a damned *hat.* But Bertie had said for him to cast about and come up with some names, plural. He had done so, never guessing that he would be the one to present them to the wily, audacious wid— Wait—what? He found himself bracing, scrambling mentally. *Experiencing* men?

"I shall just have to see them for myself," she said calmly.

"Beg pardon?" He shook himself more alert.

"I said, I shall have to see them for myself in order to decide which to marry. Where do they live? Surely you will be able to learn that much."

"What are you proposing?" Every inch of his skin contracted. He had gooseflesh all the way down to his John Thomas.

"To visit these men, compare them and perhaps…sample a kiss."

"The devil you will." He stepped closer, reaching for her before he checked that reaction and curled his hands into fists at his sides. "You cannot go gallivanting around the country demanding kisses from strange men."

"But they're not strange men. They're men who were selected for me. By *you*." She edged closer, her face raised, her eyes bright with challenge. "I doubt they would shrink from providing a sample of their amorous skill. Men are usually eager to oblige in such matters." She raked him with a look that could have ignited a wet lump of coal. "Most men, anyway."

His mouth opened, but after a moment shut. Heat was thundering through his veins. Frustration, annoyance and outrage, he told himself.

"*You* managed to survive one of my kisses." Her gaze landed on his lips as she wetted her own. "Can you honestly say it was objectionable or an imposition?"

She was mere inches away, her eyes glistening, her cheeks rosy. Her lips—soft lips that had moved with such exquisite provocation over his—were moist and succulent and so very, very near.

It was all he could do to do nothing at all.

"I thought not." Her voice seemed thicker, sultrier as she stepped back. "Then tomorrow morning we shall leave for Lincoln to find this Thomas Bickering, Esquire. You did come by coach, did you not?"

He jerked a nod, realizing only now the full scope of the task before him. He was stuck husband-hunting with a woman who had beguiled and disarmed half a dozen men hell-bent on dissipation, with nothing more than a fiddle and a punch bowl. She was striking, sensual, self-possessed and had already proven she had as much command over his body as he did.

"Excellent." She caught his gaze and held it in triumph. "While there you can visit Barclay's Bank and arrange the funds to cover my note."

She paused, waiting for a response that he refused to give her. With a growl, he turned on his heel and headed for the door.

"Cheer up, Jack B. Nimble." The satisfaction in her voice scraped his broad back like cat's claws. "By tomorrow night you might be celebrating my upcoming nuptials."

# 5

A GLOSSY, black-lacquered coach arrived at the front door of the inn the next morning at nine in sunny weather that belied the tightening chill of the season. Mariah sent her trunk out with Old Robert while she waited in the hall with Mercy, whom she had drafted to accompany her.

The old woman tugged at her straining jacket, grumbling that it had somehow shrunk since she wore it last. Mariah smoothed her own navy woolen skirt, resettled her military-style jacket at her waist, and drew her kidskin gloves higher on her wrists. After a moment, she stepped back to check herself in the hall mirror. The vivid blue of her eyes and pink of her cheeks surprised her. She was positively glowing.

*Stop that,* she ordered herself.

An instant later, the sunlight coming through the open door dimmed. She looked over to find Jack St. Lawrence's tall, broad-shouldered form silhouetted against the brightness. Her heart dropped a beat.

"A steamer trunk?" His irritation seemed to push some of the air out of the hall as he leaned inward.

"Who knows how long we'll be gone?" she said, forcing a deep breath as she retrieved her reticule and lap blanket from the hall table.

"One and a half days," he declared. "Thirty hours, give or take. How many changes of clothing can you possibly need in thirty hours?"

He was eager to be rid of her. Too blessed bad. She was in no hurry to select one of the men on his list as her lord and master. Her only hope, she had realized, was to draw out the process either until she could find someone she could bear to marry or until she exhausted the prince's patience without simultaneously invoking his wrath.

"That is an absurd time estimate under the best of circumstances," she said. "Should Mr. Bickering prove suitable, there will be certain formalities to conduct, some of which may require days to complete. To say nothing of the shopping that will be required."

"Shopping?" His horror was palpable.

"I believe the baron mentioned new clothing." She lowered her voice and gestured to her serviceable but uninspired skirt and jacket. "I simply cannot undertake my new role in such garments. *And* should Mr. Bickering prove unsuitable, we shall have to go on to the next candidate."

Muttering something unintelligible, he turned and stalked down the steps to the coach. When she approached the vehicle with Mercy in tow, he suddenly registered the old girl's hat and traveling gear.

"What's *this?*" He looked to Mariah in exasperation.

"My maid." She met his incredulity full-on. "A respectable woman never travels without assistance."

Mercy lifted her chins with exaggerated dignity and held out a hand for assistance in mounting the steps. Jack first extended his arm and then hefted and grappled and finally pushed her substantial frame through the door. Red-faced, he collected himself and then helped Mariah up.

Mercy, unused to coach travel, had ensconced herself on the forward-facing seat. Mariah settled beside her without correcting her gaffe, leaving the rear-facing seat for Jack, who bit his tongue, settled back against the tufted leather, and rapped the upholstered roof of the coach with his walking stick. The vehicle lurched forward, pulling a gasp and giggle from Mercy.

As it happened, Mariah needn't have bothered with the lap blanket; the sun coming through the windows warmed the coach...too well. The smell of naphtha soon permeated the air, courtesy of Mercy, who had pulled her traveling clothes out of storage only that morning. The combination of riding backward and the smell of mothballs soon had Jack looking a little green. He let down one of the windows for some fresh air and it wasn't long before Mariah was spreading that lap blanket after all.

"Never been all th' way to Lincoln." Mercy gawked out the window as they rolled past dun-colored fields bounded by meandering stone walls and clusters of cottages with smoke curling out of squat stone chimneys. "The old squire stayed to home. Said he'd done his travelin'. At least, after Miz Mariah come. A'fore that, he went to Lincoln regular an' come home all wrung out, like he—"

"Mercy," Mariah said with an edge, hoping to head off a trip down memory lane, "are you cold?"

"Naw. Got my quilties on." She looked to Jack. "He was with East Inja Comp'ny, ye know. That's how come we got them fancy rugs all over."

"I hadn't noticed," Jack said, glancing at Mariah as if to say it was her fault he was having to listen to this.

"Brung 'em back from Inja," Mercy continued. "Them an' all kinds o' swords and shields and trunks of feathers an' oils. Alwus had 'is nose in a book. 'Til Miz Mariah come. Then—" she grinned "—he didn't have no time fer books. Couldn't take 'is eyes off *her.*"

"*Really,* Mercy," Mariah said, betraying a touch of anxiety, which she quickly banished. "I'm sure Mr. St. Lawrence isn't interested."

"Oh, but I am," Jack protested. "What sort of man was the squire?"

"A right handsome bloke in 'is day." Mercy ignored Mariah's annoyance. "Tall, but not spare. Silver hair. Had standards, he did. And 'habits.' Cook said he alwus liked his brandy *before* an' his—"

"Mercy!" Mariah snapped, drawing a look of astonishment from the old woman. "You mustn't bore Mr. St. Lawrence with servants' prattle."

"Don't underestimate my tolerance for gossip, Mrs. Eller. I am enthralled." He gave Mercy a smile that set her preening. "Go on."

"He were a bach'lor fer years." Mercy chuckled. "Said, why pick one flower when there wus a whole garden to enjoy?"

"A common enough sentiment," Jack said. "What changed his mind?"

Mariah groaned silently. Mercy was past all caution, and the last thing she needed was Jack poking around in her marriage.

"The mistress, o' course. Went off to Lincoln one day, like always, and come home days later with a bride. Said it were like he wus hit by lightning. Struck by her beauty, he was."

Beauty indeed. Mariah reddened. She didn't like where this was headed: a mythologized tale of their meeting that her husband had concocted to tease her and satisfy the servants' curiosity.

"Her pa had just died, an' Lord knew, th' squire was needin' a wife. Wasted no time, old Mason. Like a kid with Christmas peppermints. Married her the next day." Mercy cast a mischievous grin at her. "Little bitty slip o' a thing, Miz Mariah. Hardly said a word for days."

"Doesn't sound like her," he said with a glance Mariah's way.

The old woman chuckled, ignoring her mistress's "tsk" of warning.

"Gentle-raised, she was. Squire had to teach her everthin'."

*"Everything?"* Jack propped both hands on the head of his walking stick, looking Mariah over. "A patient man, indeed."

"Everthin' about—"

"Mercy, it will be several hours before we reach Lincoln," Mariah inserted firmly. "You should rest while you have the chance."

Reading in her mistress's glare that her moment was over, Mercy nestled back in her corner, sighed with resignation and closed her eyes. Soon she was snoring softly and Mariah was able to breathe easier. Despite the draft from the open window, she began feeling warmer and tucked her lap blanket around the old servant.

When she looked up, Jack was studying her.

"How old was he—your husband?" he asked.

Curse Mercy for stirring up his curiosity.

"Older."

"How much older?" His gaze intensified.

"I hardly think that is relevant here." She pulled a small writing pad and pencil out of her purse. "Tell me, what is the prince's favorite color?"

"You married him after a day? A precipitously short courtship."

"That seems to be my fate." She concentrated on her pad and tried to change the subject. "I thought perhaps I should include some of the prince's favorites in my wardrobe. Is he more of a satin or a damask man?"

"Your father had died, so who arranged the marriage?" He leaned forward.

"A magistrate who decided I needed a husband."

"Needed?" His brows rose.

"I had nowhere else to go," she said flatly. "The magistrate introduced us and the squire made me an offer of marriage then and there."

"How old were you?"

"Old enough."

He thought on that, drawing heaven knew what kind of conclusions. She hated the feeling of being weighed and palpated like a holiday goose.

"And you were married for how long?" he continued.

"It's a bit late to be examining my credentials, is it not?"

"Ten years? A dozen?" he prodded.

"Over seven." Long, eventful years that she had success- fully locked away…feathers, oils and all. Until a week ago.

"During which time he *taught* you things." He sat forward, looking her over with those unusual amber-colored eyes. Clearly, he did not intend to be diverted. Curse him. There was nothing more tenacious than a man on the trail of a woman's vulnerability.

"My husband was a man of many facets." Her face warmed as she clung to hard-won composure. "As, I am sure, is the prince. His Highness is fond of music, obviously. What else is he fond of?"

Jack smiled in a way that made her want to retract the question.

"Women," he said without altering his intense regard. "Was your husband fond of them, too?"

His aggressive posture and the speculation in his face pushed her discomfort to its limits. But the cracks in her own composure suddenly allowed her to see the weaknesses in his. He was a man who liked to be in control…of a situation, of himself. Why else would he be the only one sober at the end of an evening's revelry with the prince?

"Quite so, Mr. St. Lawrence." Control. She knew all about men who had to be in control. She slid into the bold, unflappable part of her being that had allowed her to handle Mason's demands without quailing. She leaned forward to call Jack's arrogance and raise him a bit of self-assurance.

"In fact, my husband was something of a connoisseur of women. He had lived in the Orient, you see, where pleasures of the flesh are considered normal and even desirable."

Jack sensed something had changed and he froze, mid-coach, eye to eye with her.

There was that word again. *Pleasures.* She was leaning toward him now, meeting his gaze dead-on, the stormy blue of her eyes like whirlpools ready to drag the unwary male under the surface of duty and respectability and into oblivion. But what a demise it would be...giving in to the erotic urges that had seized him that night at the inn...drowning in his own juices...yielding to his own reckless, consuming...

"Colors?" she reminded him, smiling coolly.

"I have no earthly idea." Every muscle in his body tensed as he sat back and wished the seat were in a different coach and headed in the opposite direction from wherever *she* was going.

"Surely you've seen him express some preference."

"Not really."

"Then the choice of his own clothes may provide a clue."

"Plaid," he said shortly. "Royal tartan. Gray, tan and black."

The blasted woman was going about this like a damned business: studying her new protector, devising god-knew-what snares and temptations for the unsuspecting wretch, making no bones about her purely pecuniary interest in his attentions. Worse: dragging *him* into her plotting.

"Then perhaps fragrances. What scents does he favor?"

"Soap. He always smells of *soap*. And cigars."

"Hmmm. I doubt I'll find eau de cigar in a perfumer's shop." She tapped her lips, drawing his attention to that plump, rosy flesh…fashioned into extravagant bow-shaped curves… "Flowers?"

"I have no bloody idea what—*gardens,* he likes gardens," he said curtly, crossing his arms and glancing out the window. "Goes on and on about the fine gardens at this or that house." He gave a grimace of a smile. "Perhaps you could smear a little garden dirt behind each ear."

"Dirt behind the ears," she muttered dutifully as she wrote on her pad. He dragged his walking stick across his knees and gripped the ends of it like a fighting staff, knowing it was useless in this sort of battle.

"What do you think—is he more visual or tactile?" When he scowled, she clarified, "Is he a *looker* or a *toucher?*" Holding her pencil poised, she appeared thoughtful. "He seemed to like having his hands in my hair."

"It's not for me to say," he bit out, filled with images and indignation.

"I only ask because you are my sole source of information, and it has a direct impact on what sort of garments I buy. Some men like to see a woman's bounty grandly and brazenly displayed. Others prefer to have to peel away layers of frilly armor to reveal a woman's intimate secrets."

*A woman's bounty…frilly armor…intimate secrets…* Every word was an incantation conjuring salacious images in his head.

"This entire line of questioning is beyond the pale," he said, outrage compressed into every syllable. "This is my future king. Speaking of him in such a manner is…is *indecent.*"

"No more indecent than being sent to procure a woman for him, surely," she said with an edge so fine that it drew blood without him noticing at first. "And yet, you seemed to have no difficulty with that."

"That is an en-entirely different matter," he sputtered, his face on fire.

"Because it was a mere woman's decency being presumed upon? I can see why you make such distinctions. You must surely see why I cannot."

Arrogant female, equating her honor to their future king's! Yet, even as he thought it, his pricked conscience winced at the comparison. This was not the middle ages, where *le droit de seigneur* was the universal right of lords. He shook himself. For God's sake, it was the Prince of Wales, heir to their nation's throne and empire. Surely she could see that his needs—

That word brought him up short. *Needs?* It was more a matter of privilege, he had to concede. Heaven knew the prince had no needs that hadn't long ago been filled to surfeit. The prince's desires, then—it should be an honor to serve them. And it wasn't as though she wouldn't be recompensed.

"Very well." She broke the silence and made a note on her pad. "You refuse to discuss the prince's preferences, so I shall just have to be guided by your own."

"Mine?" His grip on his walking stick and his jaw both loosened.

"As a representative. Most certainly. You hunt together, attend the same functions and admire the same fashionable ladies, do you not? Then what appeals to you must, by all logic, appeal to him."

He was speechless with disbelief and experiencing an alarming rush of anticipation. She was going to use him as a stand-in for Bertie! And in so doing, she was going to punish him for the sin of denying her the kiss she had expected on that first night…for keeping his mouth shut when he should have spoken the truth…for handing her over to the prince… and for coercing her into a liaison she claimed not to want.

In short, she was going to make him pay for every scorched inch of her flaming pride.

Jack dropped his walking stick, jammed his shoulders into the corner of the coach, and stretched his legs out across the seat beside him. Jaw set, he tilted his hat down over his face and crossed his arms to close off further discussion.

She wasn't so easily dismissed.

"So, Jack St. Lawrence—" her voice lowered and lapped around his tensed body in warm, suggestive waves "—in intimate situations, do you prefer to see a woman arrayed in permissive silk lingerie or cinched into stern-boned corsets and twenty-button gloves?"

His teeth ground together. He squeezed his eyes tighter and his whole body tensed. Provocative flashes of nipples veiled by translucent silk and breasts bulging above black satin boning flared in his mind. Punishment indeed. The silk in his vision slid…the corset loosened…blue eyes burned and wine-sweetened lips beckoned…tempting and accusing him. Hypocrite. Denying himself in the name of duty. Denying her in the name of his own damnable—

With a growl he sat upright, slammed his hat on the seat, and in one swift move was across the coach and grabbing her by the shoulders. He pulled her to him and smothered her shocked "What—oh—" with a blistering kiss that softened into an exploration as it went on and on…warming, absorbing, caressing…until her resistance melted and his sanity and self-possession were unrecognizable lumps simmering in a stew of desire.

Somewhere in the throes of it, he sank onto one knee in the foot well and leaned into her, trapping her legs between the seat and his body. Her mouth fitted itself to his, drawing him closer and deeper into the kiss. Sweet—her lips were faintly sweet, just as he had recalled—and moist and warm.

Her silky tongue was tentative at first in its movements, then more assured, as if she were remembering how to cast that particular spell.

Her shoulders were firmer under his hands than he would have expected, and that thought fired his curiosity about the rest of her. Shapely and strong; the combination surprised and intrigued him. Suddenly everything in the images he'd conjured—bare skin and taut nipples and reddened lips—belonged to her. And there she was at his fingertips, warming to him, willing to—

A snuffling snort and some movement on the seat beside them punched through the steam in his senses. He drew back the same instant she did and in a heartbeat was braced against the opposite seat, breathing hard, his skin too tight and his muscles twitching in protest.

The snoring Mercy smacked her lips dryly in her sleep and shifted so that her cheek lodged against the wall of the coach. He could barely swallow as he watched the old girl settle back into sleep. Relieved, he yanked down his vest and made himself meet Mariah's questioning look.

Her eyes were wide and her lips were swollen from his kiss. Without a single hair out of place, she managed to look tousled and ready for more. This—this desire, this turmoil—was what it would have been like if he had kissed her that night.

"Now you know," he managed, struggling to justify his impulse.

If the avowed motivation for his action shocked her, she hid it well.

"So I do. It seems the prince is quite a kisser." She responded after a moment with a tight little smile and coolly raised her pad and began to make notes. As she concentrated, the tip of her tongue emerged to stroke her kiss-reddened lips—the very territory his had covered moments earlier. Sweet Jesus. He slammed his eyes shut against the sight.

She was making notes on his kiss.

# 6

MARIAH had time as the coach wound through the chilled countryside to recover her determination to ignore Jack St. Lawrence's arrogance. And attractions. Which were sprawled with masculine aplomb in front of her.

He was so smug in his male autonomy. No one told *him* who to bed. How could he possibly understand how demeaning it was for a woman to be considered available for *use* by a man, even a prince?

As unappetizing as the thought of passion with the portly prince was, it was the marriage part that really stung. A part of her had begun to hope that a new love would walk into her inn and into her life…someone who could make her heart sing and body yearn…someone with whom she could share bed and board and the passing years. But the prince's insistence that she marry for *his* convenience put that dream out of reach forever.

She thought of Thomas Bickering. How likely was he to be tall, clean-limbed and athletic looking, with thick, run-your-fingers-through-me hair and a simmering gaze that made her body hot and tingly? Not very.

If only she could go back to her simple life and her uncomplicated hopes.

But she knew better. The minute Jack's touch reminded her she was a woman, that time of healing and illusion of simplicity was over.

This was the hand that Fortune had dealt her. She had to find a way to navigate its trials and temptations and make a new life for herself. And what if this mistress debacle was itself an instrument of Fate? What if she was meant to start again with one of the potential husbands she met on this journey? She pulled Jack's list from her purse and stared at the names with an ache around her heart: men who would marry a prince's mistress for favor and financial gain. She took a deep breath.

Something told her she'd best prepare for the worst.

The coach slowed sometime later, and she leaned to the window. They had entered a stream of traffic approaching the city.

The change in motion awakened Jack; he stirred, sat up and stretched. His eyes had the heaviness of a man fresh from bed and his dark hair was mussed just enough to make him seem appealingly vulnerable. Accessible. Fortunately, Mercy awoke as well and complained that sleeping twisted like a corkscrew had set her joints aching.

"Whew!" The old woman wrinkled her nose. "What's that smell?"

Apparently, it was Lincoln. Everything about the city, a medieval cathedral town and woolen center whose fortunes had risen and fallen through the centuries, was washed a smelly, sooty gray. Mariah winced as she imagined living in a place where the air had a color and carried a perpetual tang of iron and oil. Lincolnshire's seat had come alive once more with the development of Britain's industrial might, but at a price.

They stopped first at the White Hart Hotel in Bailgate, near the cathedral, to secure lodgings and learn where they might find the legal firm employing Thomas Bickering. The manager of the venerable brick inn directed them to a district where banks and solicitor firms were located.

Leaving Mercy at the hotel to settle her things into her room, Mariah set off with Jack to find Yarborough Street.

"I'll go in first," Jack said, rigid now and curt, "and tell him—"

"Nothing," she countered, having to work to keep up with his long strides. "You'll not say a word about why we are here. I need to see what sort of man he is apart from royal bribes."

"I should think that would already be more than plain," he bit out. "He's the kind of man who seizes an opportunity when it presents itself."

She halted on the pavement, sensing that he'd revealed something about himself. When he realized she had stopped, he turned to look at her.

"Like you?" Sharpening her gaze, she tried to slice through the male bluster of duty to crown and country to glimpse the man beneath. "I've been wondering, Jack, what do you get out of this? What opportunity does settling a royal mistress in the prince's bed open for *you?*"

He reddened, and a muscle flexed in his jaw. Without a word he turned and struck off down the street again.

Well. She stood watching his broad shoulders trying to shake off some of the conflict they carried. He seemed to have a conscience after all. He knew that the position they'd forced her into wasn't right. It didn't change anything, but that discovery felt like a small victory.

They soon found a firm called Halliwell, Soames, Makepeace and Bickering; it turned out to be just a few doors away from a stationer's shop where they stopped to inquire. The clerk, an older woman, said that the shop supplied office materials to the firm and, without being asked, revealed that Thomas Bickering had just been made a partner there.

Jack thanked her and turned to go, but Mariah lingered to

purchase some new pencils and another writing pad, and asked the clerk if she were acquainted with Mr. Bickering.

"I am. A fine young man." There was genuine admiration in the woman's eyes. "Alwus tips 'is hat to women...ladies and shop girls alike."

"A ringing endorsement from the shop-girl contingent," Jack muttered as he held the door for Mariah.

"A woman could do worse than a man who is polite to people of all stations." She shot him a look as she stepped onto the street.

Thomas Bickering's name had just been added to the sign hanging above the pavement, painted onto a board tacked below the names of the other partners. Mariah's pulse picked up as she stared at the change. At least Mr. Bickering was clever enough to advance in his chosen career.

The lobby of the firm's offices gave an impression of solidity and worth...wooden paneling, large windows and comfortable leather chairs in a waiting area set off from the clerks' desks by a heavy railing. The young man at the desk in the reception area confirmed that Thomas Bickering was indeed a member of the firm and was at that moment on the premises.

Mariah gave him her sunniest smile.

"We have it on the best authority—the Earl of Chester— that Mr. Bickering is a very capable solicitor. We've had something of a journey and are anxious to meet with him." When the clerk looked doubtful, she handed him their calling cards. "Surely he can find a few minutes in his schedule for us. The work must be started today if it is to be finished in time for the wedding." She glanced at Jack, who looked as if he were biting his tongue.

"I'll see if Mr. Bickering has some time to give you." The clerk looked from her to Jack and then down at their names.

"And may I offer sincerest congratulations. Matrimony seems to be in the air these days."

As the fellow strode off, Jack leaned closer with a glower.

"You know, you've made him think *we're*—" He cut off that alarming thought. "Do you always play so fast and loose with the truth?"

"I prefer to think of it as creative use of the facts," she countered in an emphatic sotto voce. "I can hardly barge in, demand an accounting of his personal life and then tell him he's been instructed to marry me." She looked up with a taunting smile. "That's *your* job."

The clerk returned to usher them down a hallway with: "You're in luck. Mr. Bickering has a most important engagement this afternoon, but he has agreed to see you for a few moments."

Mariah held her breath as she entered her potential husband's office.

Thomas Bickering was a man in his thirties, moderately tall and of medium build, with brown, prematurely graying hair. He looked a bit frazzled, sitting behind a large desk in an office full of crates, boxes and half-filled bookshelves. His new office, no doubt. As he rose to greet them she assessed his face—pleasant, if a little ordinary; his eyes—clear and watchful; and his handshake—firm and businesslike. He invited them to be seated in the chairs the clerk scurried to pull from under stacks of papers.

"Well, Miss Eller—" He tugged his cuffs self-consciously.

"It's Mrs. Eller," Mariah said sweetly. "I'm a widow."

"Oh." Flustered slightly, he cast about on his chaotic desktop for paper and a pen. "Well, then, this makes more sense. A second marriage. Property involved, is there?"

"I knew the earl wouldn't steer us wrong," Mariah said, putting a hand on Jack's sleeve. "You see how quickly he's assessed the situation?"

"And you—" he consulted Jack's card for his name "—Mr. St. Lawrence. Have you been married before?"

"I have not, b-but—"

"Mr. St. Lawrence has numerous properties and family to whom he has made certain promises," she inserted. "We felt it only prudent to discuss the situation with someone knowledgeable and seek professional advice."

"A wise course of action," Bickering said, smiling with fresh warmth at Mariah. He had a nice smile; his countenance became quite attractive when it appeared. She experienced a quiver of feminine interest. "If only more people would be so rational upon entering into marriage. It is, after all, a solemn responsibility as well as a joyous undertaking."

"So it is." Mariah studied the man, trying to square that statement with his presence on a list of potential husbands for a prince's mistress. *A joyous undertaking.* Perhaps there was more to him than met the eye.

"I own an inn on the Edinburgh Road, north of Lincoln, which I wish to continue to operate after my marriage," she said with a sidelong glance at Jack. "Though I will likely be spending time away from it."

"Moving to your husband's home, no doubt," Bickering said, looking increasingly uncomfortable under Jack's increasingly stony regard.

"Yes, but there are circumstances—" She laid a hand on Jack's sleeve again. "Would you mind leaving us for a few moments? I have a matter to discuss with Mr. Bickering in private."

"Private?" Jack straightened. "Anything you have to say can be said in front of me."

"I would draw on Mr. Bickering's experience in a delicate matter." She ordered him to the door with her eyes, eager to test the new sense of *possibilities* that had come over her.

Perhaps…just perhaps…being married again wasn't the worst thing that could happen to her.

"All the more reason I should be here." He scowled, clearly offended by the notion of personal contact between her and her prospective husband.

"Don't be silly, it has nothing to do with you. I simply want to consult Mr. Bickering's *experience*." She pulled Jack up by the arm and bustled him out. When she had closed the door behind him, she leaned back against it, facing Thomas Bickering, who had risen with them and stood watching her with visible confusion.

She smiled.

"Tell me, Mr. Bickering, do you think marriage is a wise choice for a woman of independent means?"

"The right marriage, Mrs. Eller. Certainly." His confusion melted into heartfelt sincerity. "The right marriage is far more than a civil arrangement for providing heirs and apportioning property. It is a partnership of souls crafted out of love, respect and commitment. As such, it is one of the greatest gifts life has to offer." His gaze shifted and warmed subtly, as if he were seeing something not quite material. "Had I believed otherwise, I would never have asked my sweet Cynthia to marry me."

"Your—" her jaw dropped "—Cynthia?"

OUT IN THE hallway, Jack St. Lawrence paced and fumed. If there hadn't been so many people around, clerks trundling back and forth with arms full of legal folios, he'd have had his ear to the lock. Why did lawyers have to have such damned thick doors?

But he didn't really have to hear; he already knew what she was up to. He could see it as plain as day in his mind. She was swaying across the room…removing her scented gloves with mesmerizing leisure…gliding around the poor wretch's desk like the Serpent in the Garden…all while interrogating him suggestively about his table manners and gambling habits and corset preferences. He could guess what came after that: a sampling of the wretch's amorous skill. Or lack thereof.

He made himself take one deep breath and another before he lunged for the knob…and managed to stop himself. Charging back inside would be tantamount to admitting that he cared that she threw herself at the lawyer. The satisfaction that would give her would be just too humiliating. Growling quietly, he stepped away from the door.

Voices rose after a few minutes and the door opened, startling him away from the wall where he had been leaning. The lawyer escorted Mariah out with a chummy hand on her elbow. Her gaze was lowered, but she was smiling, and Bickering's face was red and his eyes were unnaturally bright. Clearly, something had happened between them.

"Good to meet you, St. Lawrence. Let me know if I can be of further service." The lawyer offered Jack his hand while consulting his pocket watch. "Must be on my way. Can't afford to be late—not for this."

With a gracious nod, he abandoned them to rush down the hall, retrieve his hat and exit via a side door. By the time Jack turned back to Mariah, she was moving in the other direction, headed for the reception area, straightening her hat and donning her gloves as she went.

He waited until they were on the street and walking briskly in the direction of the hotel before demanding, "Well?"

She looked as if she was concentrating on something as she stopped abruptly on the pavement.

"Chocolate," she declared. "I'm dying for a piece of chocolate." Peering up and down the street, she spotted something that looked like a sweet shop down the way and struck off for it.

"What?" He was caught flat-footed.

She wanted chocolate? Now?

*Infernal female.*

He followed her into a shop that specialized in gustatory decadence. The air reeked of edible sin—melting sugar and tempering chocolate—and the place was crowded with ornate glass cases containing confections displayed like the blessed Crown Jewels. She selected piece after piece of chocolate-covered nuts, nougats, crèmes and caramels. After the clerk had assembled a sizeable collection into a pink pasteboard box, she instructed the woman to give the bill to Jack, seized the package, and exited the shop.

When he caught up with her, she had pulled out a nougat the size of a Yorkshire pudding and was nibbling it. He stepped in front of her to block her way, and she looked up with lips laced with chocolate and eyes luminous with pleasure. Wordless, she held up the candy to offer him a bite.

"I want—" His mouth was watering so profusely that he had to swallow in order to speak. "I want to know what happened with Bickering."

She popped the rest of the piece into her mouth and closed her eyes, radiating such indecent pleasure that two men passing by slowed to leer at them. It was all he could do to keep from shaking her. Or licking her. Odds were even on which.

"A-are you marrying him or not?" He tried to keep his voice down.

"Not." She dabbed the corners of her mouth with the crumpled candy paper, gave an enormous sigh, and headed toward the hotel.

"Not?" The news struck him like a blast of fresh air. His

whole body relaxed. Annoyed by his relief, he hurried after her. "Why not?"

The look she gave him from the corner of her eye was infuriating. She was tormenting him and, from every indication, enjoying it.

"The hotel man indicated that there were dressmakers and milliners in the next street," she said with a wave in that direction. "I really should have a look before we leave tomorrow morning. Their work may not be quite London quality, but I imagine they'll have some things of interest."

"We're not going anywhere until I have a straight answer from you." Glancing around and finding the street around them mostly empty, he snagged her arm as they approached the hotel. "Why did you reject him?"

"Does it matter? We simply go on to the next candidate."

"Not until I know why you refuse to wed this one," he demanded.

"Very well." She tugged her arm free. "He was genial, gentlemanly, intelligent, mannerly…perfect in all respects but one."

"And that was?" He could think of only one criterion just now, staring at her chocolate-tainted lips and imagining her using them on the accommodating lawyer.

"He's being married this Saturday to the daughter of the head of his firm." Her face sobered. "Which I believe makes him ineligible as a husband for me. I don't know where you got his name, but he's been betrothed for more than a month now. And to a young woman he dearly…well, he seems to be quite smitten with her."

Cutting off further discussion, she quickened her pace to the hotel, past the doorman and through the lobby. With the box of chocolates dangling from one hand and her skirts held primly in the other, she swept up the stairs. He had to take the steps two at a time to catch up with her on the second-floor landing.

"Did you find out he was to be married before or after you kissed him?" he demanded with an urgency that should have embarrassed him. But his heart was pounding, his vision narrowing and his head was filling with the scent of the chocolate on her breath.

"A moot point, I believe." There was a trace of something like regret in her voice as she sidestepped him to continue to her room.

Determined to have an answer, he bounded up the stairs and down the hall to plant himself in her path yet again. What was it about the woman that incited him to such extremes? He'd never behaved like this with a female in his life—brash, irritable, impulsive. *Get hold of yourself, man!*

Standing over her, he clenched his hands and made himself swallow.

"Well?"

For a moment she stared straight ahead, visually scorching his shirtfront, then raised her face to him.

"Did you kiss him?" he demanded.

"What do you care?" Her eyes, dark-centered in the dim hallway, sought his. Whatever she saw in him caused her to smile in a way that melted the bones in his knees. "Unless, of course, you would prefer to be kissing me yourself." Her eyes crinkled at the corners. Lights in their depths twinkled. "Which would be perfectly understandable, after this morning. I'm a delectable kisser."

His gaze dropped to her lips and his mouth opened and then closed soundlessly. With her words ringing in his head like a bell, he managed to make himself take a step backward and allow her to pass.

It was a mistake to watch her walk away, he knew, but he couldn't take his eyes off the sway of her hips, the curve of her spine, and the errant curls at the nape of her neck. He was suddenly galvanized by the memory of the feel and the taste of her.

Like a spectator inside his own head, he saw himself go after her, turn her and swoop down on her mouth.

# 7

THERE WAS no squeal, no gasp, not so much as a breath of resistance as he bore her back into the shelter of the nearest door frame. Her lack of shock hinted that she had expected this. The way her arms lapped around his neck said she had wanted it, too.

Plunging into the taste of chocolate, the velvet of her mouth, and the responsiveness of her tongue, he found himself instantly detached from the moorings of his life… adrift…suspended in time and place. Suddenly there was no *before* or *after;* this contact, these sensations were all that existed. His body caught fire and unbidden, he wrapped both arms around her, lifting her, holding her fiercely against him, kissing her with a hunger he had forgotten he possessed.

The door behind her opened unexpectedly, and his embrace was all that kept her from falling backward through it. A man's shocked face appeared briefly through the haze in his vision, and then the door closed with a resounding thud. Operating with only a fraction of his faculties, he managed to turn her, shift them both across the narrow hall and work the knob of another door. When it opened, he carried her into the room with him, stifling the question of whose room they'd entered, and pressed her back against the wall, kicking the door shut.

Her body molded to his as he leaned into her, and her hands cupped the back of his head to pull him closer. Her mouth was alternately tender and yielding, then firm and demanding as she sought new combinations of position and pressure against his. The play of her tongue inside his lips, and the way she raked his lips with her teeth sent voluptuous sensations spiraling through him. Her words were no boast; she *was* a delectable kisser.

He could have stayed there for hours, immersed in kissing, licking and tasting her, feeling as if together they had just invented that oral entree into pleasure, but there was so much more of her to experience. He trailed his lips down the side of her face to her throat, kissing, nibbling and registering that her head sank to the side to give him access. The sight of her tongue laving her lips, compensating for the absence of his, sent a bolt of electricity through him.

His arousal was full-blown and urgent and his hands burned with the need to feel her bare skin.

THIS was what she wanted, Mariah thought, pushing aside all other thought as she leaned into Jack's body and luxuriated in the pleasure spreading along the underside of her skin. This was what he'd denied her that first night…this erotic resonance…this tingling in her lips, drawing hunger in her breasts and gathering fullness in her sex.

His hands slid over her hungrily, tracing the rim of her corset and the mounds above it. She stretched, hoping to give him access to the nipples tucked into the edge of the boning, but found herself too respectably wedged inside it. With a moan of frustration, she slipped her hands between them and he inched back—without abandoning her lips—to give her room.

"Buttons," she whimpered as she worked them with trembling fingers, "too many buttons." When her jacket opened, she realized there was another whole rank of them at her back and looked over her shoulder with a groan.

With a wicked laugh against her throat, he peeled the jacket down her arms and tossed it to the side. Before she could catch his hands and direct them to the rest of her buttons, he slid them down her hips and thighs and began reeling up her skirt and petticoat. He dipped so that his fingers could find the tops of her garters, then glide up her sensitive thighs to the frothy silk of her knickers. He muttered something vehemently appreciative.

The feel of her legs bared to the cool air was deliciously erotic. His hands, hot on her naked thighs, set off fireworks in her that shot sparks along forgotten sensory paths. Her nerves were awakening, her muscles warming with memory, her nipples and sex tingling to awareness. Her skin was aching for touch. Closer, she needed to be closer. She pressed against him, meeting his kiss, offering—demanding—more.

Reading her desire, he cupped the backs of her thighs and lifted her, holding her to him as he thrust his body against hers. She felt the ridge of his arousal against her and, with a soul-deep sigh, parted her legs.

He moved again, this time pressing more tightly, arching with uncanny precision. Vibrations from that bone-melting contact spread outward along her nerves, causing her to tilt her pelvis to a better fit. His next movement sent shudders of pleasure through them both. He knew exactly how to move his sex across hers to produce those intense, heart-stopping sensations.

"Again," she breathed against his lips. When he thrust against her, she said on a groan, "Again."

Each stroke built her excitement higher and soon she felt a quickening rush building in her. Again…again…she shuddered with pleasure…almost…almost…*almost*…

Release broke over her like an avalanche. She stiffened and gasped as the boundaries of her senses dissolved, her arms clamped fiercely around his ribs, and her muscles seized. For a long, scintillating moment she was unable to breathe, move or respond further. Then as aftershocks of pleasure shook her, she wrenched the rear of his shirt out of his trousers and ran her hands up his bare back, savoring the lean bands of muscle she found.

Something banged into the door beside them; the sound was like a rifle shot in the charged air around them. Holding her breath, she looked up into his dusky features and need-darkened eyes, then around them at the room they'd invaded. It looked familiar, but there was no sign of luggage and many of the sleeping rooms were similarly shaped and furnished. The knob rattled impatiently and there was a metallic scraping at the lock—at which he jolted aside to block the door with a shoulder and left her sliding down the wall like soggy wallpaper.

"Miz?" A knock sounded on the door. "You there, Miz Mariah? That's odd. I thought I left it open."

*Mercy.* Mariah frantically smoothed her rumpled skirts and rushed across the room to the mirror over the washstand, where she tidied her hair and stared in shock at her kiss-swollen lips. Jack's reflection in the mirror showed him red-faced and grim, with his hand on the doorknob. With a glance at her, he stepped back to admit Mercy bearing a mischievous smile and a dented box of chocolates.

"Lookit, miz, at what I found while I wus comin' back from the necessary." She held up the box, pried open one corner, and inhaled the heady aroma of the confections. "Jus' laying in the hall, it was."

"There it is." Mariah had hastily poured a basin of cool water and splashed her face. Now she turned with a towel in her hand, dabbing her damp, rosy cheeks. "We bought those earlier and I—I must have dropped them in my hurry to—get to the room."

Mercy caught Mariah's sidelong glance and the unmistakable sound of a shoe connecting with a piece of furniture. She hitched around to find Jack stalking toward the door. She glanced with exaggerated innocence from her mistress to their escort, then attacked the ribbons on the candy box.

"Well, then. It were a good thing I come along when I did."

BLAST MERCY for having the worst timing in all of humanity. Or bless her for having the best. Mariah watched the door close behind Jack and found herself torn between a tantalizing satisfaction and a sizzling hunger for more. Her knees were weak and her sex smoldered with a viscous, slow-burning heat that she had thought she'd never feel again.

Her overwhelming reaction to Jack St. Lawrence, she told herself, had to be part sexual drought-relief and part reaction to having her marital hopes dashed just when they were starting to rise.

The tenderness in Bickering's eyes, the husky reverence in his voice as he spoke of his bride had generated a longing in her. And that dangerous yearning had roused a fear that her vulnerability to Jack St. Lawrence might not be as simple as mere lust.

She had experienced enough lust in her life—as both recipient and initiator—to know that it had never generated this intensely personal sort of pleasure, this level of *emotion* in her. She wanted to be with Jack physically, to experience her whole repertoire of delights with him, but she also wanted to tease him and watch the way he flushed in response, and to make him smile the way he had yesterday.

By the next morning, when she saw him pause in the doorway of the hotel restaurant, she knew that she was in trouble. Her heart began to pound as he crossed the room with that long, potent stride, immaculately groomed but hollow-eyed, clearly suffering the aftermath of an evening ill spent. *If only she could have ill-spent it with him.*

It was all she could do to keep from pulling him down for a blistering kiss. She pressed her lips against her teacup instead.

Now in the coach, on the way to her next matrimonial prospect, she couldn't keep her eyes off his long legs and struggled to avoid looking at the tantalizing bulge in his trousers. It was going to be a very, very long ride.

IT WAS indeed a good thing the old woman had returned to the room when she did, Jack had thought as he stalked out of the room, out of the hotel and into the nearest pub, where he sat in a darkened corner and consumed three enormous belts of Scotch in succession. He thought the same thing the next morning in the hotel breakfast room when his heart beat a regimental quick-time at the sight of Mariah Eller's nubile lips pressed against a china cup. And he thought it yet again when he was forced to accompany her and her old servant on a tour of female haberdasheries, and she insisted on having his opinion of the scent applied to a pair of black twenty-button gloves.

Infernal female. He'd barely got out of the shop before his John Thomas grew into a full-blown Jonathan Thomasville.

After shopping, she insisted on accompanying him to Barclays Bank to pay off her mortgage. By the time they climbed into the carriage and started for Grantham, he was feeling surly and put upon and irritated by his own impulses. He was stuck with her, couldn't keep his eyes off her and wanted nothing more than to snatch her up and carry her off and— And what kind of woman responded the way she did to a man's touch? She was sexually incendiary; she practically exploded in his damned arms!

It was a good thing that he hadn't had time yesterday to do more than ravish her up against a wall. Again. Lord knew what sort of conflagration might occur if he ever managed to get *horizontal* with her.

*Marry her off, man, and be done with it,* his pragmatic side demanded. *Then get on with finding your "advantageous" bride. Forget connection and pedigree...just go for money. Lots of it. So the family will leave you alone.*

An odd burning sensation made him reach up covertly to massage his chest above his heart. The special marriage license in his coat pocket rustled as his hand brushed it. He jerked away with alarm. It was like carrying a live snake in his damned pocket.

# 8

---

"WE SHOULD arrive in Grantham early in the afternoon," Jack announced as the carriage rocked along to the sound of the dozing Mercy's adenoidal distress. "We'll find an inn with a public room for you to rest while I inquire and make arrangements with the local vicar."

"A bit premature, I think, to involve the clergy," she responded.

"Not at all," he countered. "What are the odds of *two* of your prospects being married off?"

"At the risk of repeating myself, there are more things to be considered than just eligibility. I have certain standards that must be—"

He gave a snort. "The gravy-on-the-vest test."

"Well, you can tell a lot about a man from his eating habits." Her eyes narrowed, daring him to meet them. He knew better than to accept that challenge. "You for instance."

"Me?" Part of him went rigid with indignation, part of him just went rigid. Eating habits. He huffed dismissively and crossed his legs, trying to ignore the fact that his ears and his John Thomas were both itching for more.

"This morning you ate as if a wolf pack were waiting at your elbow to snatch it away." She tilted her head to study him. "You don't happen to have a raft of brothers at home, do you?"

"If you consider four a 'raft,' then I believe they qualify."

"I take it you are not the eldest," she said, her regard sharpening as it slid over him. "Nor the youngest."

"I am the third of five sons, all still very much alive and well. Not that *that* means a thing. Except that St. Lawrences come from hardy stock."

Her insightful smile said it meant more to her.

"Stuck in the middle," she mused. "Never the first, never the last. Always being pushed somewhere by someone. That explains it."

"Explains what, exactly?" He hated the way she openly analyzed things and drew conclusions that too often were dead-on.

"Your eating habits. Hurry, hurry, hurry. You don't take time to *savor*." Her gaze softened. "Have you ever slowly bitten into the yielding flesh of a warm, freshly picked peach…letting the tart flavor burst on your tongue and then turn into a sweetness that bathes your mouth and lingers for minutes afterward?" Her fingertips trailed over her chin and down her neck, carrying his gaze with them. "Ever allowed the juice to pool around your tongue and trickle lazily down your throat? Ever felt its liquid sunshine spreading warmth and vitality all through you?"

He had to clear his constricted throat.

"Food is food," he declared, sensing he was never going to look at a peach the same way again. "Not a damned religious experience."

"Some very wise men would disagree with that statement. *All* experiences, it has been said, have a spiritual component."

"Well, I can think of a few things that would challenge that notion." He pulled a sour face. "Your cook's tripe-and-turnip sandwich, for one."

She burst into laughter so clear and genuine that it was almost musical. Mercy started awake and sat up blinking. The gape on the old girl's face added to the moment and he gave in to a wry chuckle himself.

"I'll concede your point on Aggie's tripe-and-turnips, but on the greater truth I remain firm," she said, grinning. "But taking time to enjoy the small pleasures—food and drink, music, color, symmetry, texture—contributes to a sense of balance, and thus to a long, healthy life." Her mirth muted to a warmth that clutched at something in his chest. "What do you enjoy, Jack St. Lawrence? Besides kissing."

"R-Really, Mrs. Eller—" He glanced from her to Mercy, horrified by the interest on the old woman's face.

"Naught to be squeamish about." Mercy grinned, showing missing teeth. "Ain't a man under eighty don't like layin' one on a handsome lass."

Only somewhat reassured that Mercy's statement had not implied knowledge of his behavior with her mistress, he tugged on his vest and shifted bum cheeks on the seat.

"Horses. I have a great interest in horses, and the mechanicals that replace them…locomotives and steam-powered carriages." He glanced at her defensively, as if expecting her to laugh. When she didn't, he found himself wanting to continue. "I am also interested in the engineering of electrical inventions like the telephone, the telegraph and streetlamps."

"So, you're a man who likes to understand the inner workings of things," she mused.

"I suppose that could be said."

"We have more in common than you might imagine. What else do you like? Clearly, you're a devotee of hunting and the 'manly' sports."

He studied her for a moment, seeing a genuine curiosity in her face, and was struck by a desire to tell her the truth.

"Not really. I confess to a love of the craftsmanship of a well-made gun, but I've never been fond of the bloody mess they make. Not overly pleased by what hounds do to foxes, either."

"And yet, you ride with the prince and hunt with him."

"Family tradition." He glanced out the window to avoid the probing of her gaze. "My elder brothers hunted with the prince. Each was tasked with the prince's well-being and served his interests. Now it's my turn."

"And your elder brothers, where are they now?" she asked.

"Settled in advantageous marriages on handsome estates." A perverse impulse made him add, "Which is where I should be soon, providing—"

He halted, horrified. He was barking mad to have revealed so much. And madder still to reveal that what he truly hunted in the prince's company was advancement via *marriage*.

"Providing you can find a suitably 'advantageous' bride?" she finished for him with an alarming spark in her eyes.

"A *proper* bride," he corrected. *Proper,* of course, meaning one who was noble or wealthy enough to add to the family prestige. It was his duty.

She studied him for what seemed an age.

"Well, it seems we're both in the market for matrimony," she said.

"We are?" Mercy, watching between them, turned to stare open-mouthed at her. "Yer gettin' married, miz? Whatever for?"

Disarmed by Mercy's blunt question and expectation of an answer, Mariah scrambled to hold on to some semblance of authority.

"There are certain…practical considerations…that require forging a new…partnership." She lifted her chin with a censuring look, but nothing short of a brickbat could have prevented the old girl's response.

"Well, why don't ye just go to one o' them bankers, like

before?" Mercy shook her head. "Ye don't have to go an' get—"

"Mercy!" Mariah's face reddened as she drew her line in the sand. "There are a *few* things in my life that are not open for discussion with you."

Mercy scowled and scratched beneath the bonnet ribbons under her chin. Then she managed to put one and one together.

"So, ye're husband huntin'? That's what's got us traipsin' all over?"

Mariah sighed tautly. "I am interviewing prospects." Then as the old girl drew breath to speak, Mariah deflated her with a glare. "And, *no,* I do not need advice, thank you."

Mercy turned to the window, her chin jutting at a stubborn angle. The way Mariah stole glances at her pouting servant made Jack reflect on what sort of woman kept old servants on past usefulness and indulged their cheek.

One who was bright enough to recognize the paradoxes of humanity. One who was complicated enough herself to know that the truth lay well beneath the surface of things. One whose vibrant, unselfconscious laughter could light up a coach. An inn. A life.

To combat the hollow, hungry feeling spreading in his chest, he leaned back into the corner of the carriage and propped his hat over his face.

*Don't think about how she makes you want to hear that laughter again. Don't think about how chocolaty she tasted and how firm and full she felt in your hands. Or about garters…silk stockings…sleek thighs…breasts spilling over a lacy corset…whatever you do, don't think about the way she responded when she parted her legs and fitted herself against your swollen John—DAMN IT!*

He groaned silently.

He was in big trouble.

THE CARRIAGE made good time on unseasonably dry and stable roads, so they arrived at the town of Grantham in time to pause for a bolstering bit of tea while Jack made inquiries as to Clapford's location.

"The house is not far down the Cambridge Road," he said with forced good humor as he escorted the women to the coach. "I have a good feeling about this one. Half an hour and your search will be over."

After he handed Mercy up the steps and turned to assist Mariah, she paused for a moment and lowered her voice.

"I've been thinking about that," she said. "To make the most of my *opportunities,* I think I should see all three of my remaining prospects before deciding." At such close range it was impossible not to notice his color drain.

"The devil, you will. That could take days, *weeks.*" He looked alarmed, then accusing. "You promised to marry within a fortnight."

"*If* I find the right man," she said, having the unsettling thought that the moment she married, his job with her was finished. As was her cherished independence, she told herself, forcing thoughts of him aside.

"Clapford is the right man. He's rich. Or soon will be."

"That's *your* criterion for a mate," she said pointedly, "not *mine.*"

He reddened, but shook off the barb.

"It's a sight more rational than the number of gravy stains on a weskit." He waved her up the carriage steps with a sweaty hand. "Trust me. You'll be a baroness-in-waiting by nightfall."

*And if I'm not?* she asked with her eyes.

His whole body flushed hot when she brushed against him on the way up the step and he felt that damned special license crinkle again.

# 9

CLAPFORD HOUSE proved to be a sizeable, plain-brick country house sitting on a knoll totally devoid of trees. The grass of what must at one time have been a proud lawn had gone to seed, and clumps of scrub growth and tall weeds grew randomly about the place. The singular feature of the house's approach was a large garden pond that had a vine-wrapped fountain at the center. Knee-deep in the pond were a man in rubber boots and three bare-legged boys with reddened hands full of weeds and muck.

As the coach drew near, Jack lowered the window and they heard the man barking orders as he pointed and sloshed about in the water.

"It's October," Mariah said, shivering at the chilled air coming through the window. "What are they doing in the pond at this time of year?"

"Freezin' their arses off," Mercy muttered, crowding in for a look.

Jack bolted down the steps the moment the coach stopped at the unadorned entrance to the house. It took prolonged and vehement banging before the knockerless door finally opened to reveal an aged houseman in the shadowy interior, blinking at the brightness surrounding Jack.

"John St. Lawrence to see Mr. Clapford. Please tell him I am here on *royal* business."

The old man sighed heavily and then pushed past Jack to trudge out across the gravel carriage turn, headed for the pond. Scowling, Jack looked back at Mariah and Mercy, who had just exited the coach with the driver's help. They caught his puzzlement and hurried over to stand with him.

"Sarr's got a visitor!" the old boy shouted hoarsely. He gave an arthritic wave and tried again. "Says 'roy-al business!'"

The man in the pond stopped shouting and stomping long enough to cup his ear toward the old houseman. *"Loyal what?"*

So the man in the pond was Clapford? Mariah thought.

*"Royal...business!"*

"Heeey, I got one!" One of the boys held up a large orange-and-black spotted fish that flopped sluggishly in the cold. "Make a fine supper!"

Clapford thunked him sharply on the top of the head.

"That's *my* fish, you git!" He pointed to a wooden barrel on the bank. "Put it in the barrel!" As Clapford stalked toward the bank he fumed, "This damned well better be important. You lot—" he motioned for the boys to stay when they started to follow him out of the water "—I didn't say you could quit. I want every fish out of this pond by the time I come back. I know exactly how many there are, and they'd better *all* be there!"

"But, it's freezin'—" The smallest boy's complaint was silenced by Clapford's glare.

The baron-to-be waded out and stalked toward them with his aged woolen frock coat and his battered boots flapping. He was tall, lean and graying, with an aesthetic mien and features pinched into a perpetual frown.

"Yes?" He stopped in front of Jack, propped his fists on his waist, and assessed Jack's fashionable appearance with suspicion. "What's this about a royal matter?" Before Jack could respond, he demanded, "Who are you? Am I supposed to know you?"

"I don't believe we've met. John St. Lawrence, at your service." Jack tipped his hat. "A friend of the Prince of Wales. And Baron Marchant."

"Marchant? That gadfly?" Clapford snorted. "The prince?" He apparently reconsidered his rudeness, for he offered a grudging nod. "What does the young reprobate want with me?"

"May I present Mrs. Mariah Eller," Jack said with a strained smile.

Clapford gave an impatient nod in her general direction.

"Bertie is very fond of gardens, you know," she inserted, striving for a pleasant tone while studying the stony, unyielding man being offered up as her husband and master.

Hardly an auspicious start, she thought as she suffered a prescient glimpse of the life that awaited the woman who became the wretch's wife. Forty years of mind-numbing misery flashed before her eyes.

Her heart sank, revealing the hope growing like a weed among her carefully cultivated defenses. Partnership. Desire. Passion. She wouldn't be having such pointless thoughts if it weren't for Bickering's sentimental ramblings on marriage.

*And Jack's revelation of his own marital ambitions.*

"Bertie is putting in a new pond at Sandringham," she said, glancing at Jack to demand support for another of her spontaneous fictions. "And he asked us to stop by and see your fish. He's heard so much about them."

"The idiots damn near let the lot die while I was gone." Clapford scowled over his shoulder at the boys shivering in the thigh-deep water. "Good thing I left London early. They'd done nothing to prepare for winter. Could lose half of my beauties before it's over."

"Not to mention a few servant boys," she added archly.

Her comment didn't earn her so much as a look, but Clapford's long nose curled on one side as if he smelled something disagreeable.

"Deserve what they get, leaving my fish to freeze." He raised his chin, addressing Jack alone. "So the prince wants some of my golden koi, does he? Well, he'll have to pay for them. This isn't the bloody middle ages, you know, when forest, fish and fowl all belonged to the crown."

"I am certain the prince would wish you to get all that is coming to you," Mariah said sweetly. "I must have a look at these 'beauties' you prize so." She pulled Mercy along with her to the pond.

Clapford didn't notice the sparks in her eyes or the force of her stride as she walked away. Jack, however, made note of both…as well as the tension in her spine and the set of her jaw. He groaned privately as he endured Clapford's ramblings about fish pedigrees and the outrage of a royal making demands on a member of parliament.

This was not going to end in matrimony. He could just tell.

Not that he could blame her. Clapford was an oaf. Pompous and irascible…had about as much humanity as a slab of granite. And what kind of lout refused even to look at a beautiful woman, much less respond to her?

Gazing past the self-absorbed near-peer, he watched Mariah examine the fish in the barrels and smile warmly as she talked to the boys. The little wretches responded eagerly to her, gazing up at her as if she were made of pure sunshine. He felt a curious tug in his chest. When she sent Mercy bustling back to the coach and the maid returned with a dented pink pasteboard box, he couldn't help a wry smile.

Clapford finally realized Jack was staring past him to the pond and hitched about to see what was taking place.

"What in infernal blazes—"

The baron-to-be went charging back down to the water to send the boys back to work. He was intercepted by Mariah, who offered him a piece of chocolate and then matched him move for move, blocking his way.

Jack could see veins popping out in Clapford's neck as Mariah refused to step aside. He winced as she turned back to the boys and insisted that each take another piece of chocolate before going back to their bone-chilling work.

Typical of her. Taking charge. Sticking her nose where it wasn't wanted. Wry pleasure washed through him. She was indeed a handful.

"A man's servants are a man's own business," Clapford declared.

"And a man's treatment of his servants is a measure of a man's character," she responded, stepping forward with her chin up, forcing him back into the water. "By which standard, sir, you are sorely lacking."

In the space of a heartbeat, Clapford brandished a fist to punctuate his response, and she—thinking she would be struck—countered with a defensive shove. Caught off guard and off balance, the future baron fell back into the cold water with a huge splash.

By the time Jack reached them, there was nothing to be done but pull Mariah away from the water and watch Clapford flail and struggle to rise—to the sound of the servant boys' laughter. Water poured down the baron's face and dripped from his coat as he staggered, cursing, onto the bank.

Jack tried to apologize, offering him a handkerchief and calling it a dreadful accident, but the baron-to-be was beyond such appeasement. He focused on Mariah with fury in his eyes and declared he'd not take such insolence from a *female*, no matter how well-connected she was.

Clapford made for her with clenched fists, but Jack stepped into his path and the future-baron confronted his broad-shouldered frame instead. Cursing, Clapford tried to push past him, but Jack grabbed and held him by his dripping coat.

"Think, man—be sensible about this," Jack growled.

The baron's fist came up…Jack's left arm shot up to block that blow and his right countered with a punch to the center of Clapford's face…and Clapford went flying back into the pond.

For a shocked moment the only sound was water lapping. Then Clapford thrashed to the surface and sat gasping in pain and holding his nose. Jack stood on the bank above him, breathing hard, his tone making the pond water seem warm by comparison.

"A bit of advice, Clapford. Never raise your hand to a lady—especially one with highly placed friends. You would find mending a broken career a great deal harder than mending a broken nose."

He stalked back to Mariah and ushered her and Mercy firmly to the coach, shouting to the driver to get underway.

No one spoke as the coach rattled down the ill-paved drive. As they made the turn onto the Cambridge Road, Mariah emerged from her shock enough to spring to the window for a look back. Mercy trampled on Jack's toes to join her. Clapford was standing in the carriage turn, shaking a fist after them. When Mariah slid back into her seat, Jack was staring at her.

"You *hit* him," she said in a shocked half whisper.

"I did. Yes." He took a deep breath, set his hat aside, and started to remove his damp gloves.

"A right proper facer, sarr." Mercy beamed fresh respect.

"He brought up a fist—I…I thought he was going to strike me," Mariah said, still trying to grasp how such a calamitous string of events could have happened. "He very nearly *did*. If you hadn't—" She paused for breath and composure. "All I did was suggest he consider the health of his servants as important as that of his blessed fish…that he show a bit of common decency."

"Expecting *common* decency from the *nobility?*" Jack's brows rose. "How eccentric of you."

"It is not ridiculous to expect people of rank and responsibility to behave with reason and restraint." She bristled. "Did you see those boys? As blue from bruises as they were from cold. Was I supposed to just stand there and let him thrash me the way he does his stable boys? Someone has to stand up to overprivileged bullies."

"Does that someone always have to be you?" he countered irritably.

*Of course it did.*

It was part of who she was, he realized, somewhat rattled by the conclusion. Standing up to arrogant, overprivileged noblemen was exactly what she would do—*what she had done that first night at the inn.*

"She's a good miztress, sarr," Mercy defended her earnestly. "Got a fair an' gen'rous heart."

She felt a personal responsibility for the people in her employ, which was why she had inserted herself into the hunting party's hazardous company. He glanced at the rotund maid whom she treated more like a dotty old aunt than a domestic. She had stood up for her people and her property and placed herself in harm's way on their behalf.

The contents of his chest felt as if they were sinking toward his knees. Despite the pain in his hand, at that moment he'd have punched a thousand vile barons on her behalf… a few hundred M.P.s…sundry earls, marquesses and dukes…even a *prince.*

His heart stopped.

Dear God. What was he thinking?

That she was a woman of substance, of surprising depths, courage and conviction. That the prince truly had gotten a mistaken notion of her character, just as she'd said. And that *he* was partly responsible.

MARIAH watched the play of strong emotions in Jack's face and guessed that he was thinking about potential consequences.

"Might this get you into trouble?" she said, feeling a stir of guilt.

"An assault on a sitting member of parliament? Whatever gives you that idea?" he said with an edge, brushing at the water spots on his trousers. "Clapford has a vile temper, but I doubt he will make an issue of this." She watched him reason it through and set aside his concern. "He won't want a report of his conduct to get around. Though it probably wouldn't come as a surprise to any who know him. Men don't lash out in anger like that unless it is from habit."

"So, he behaves that way as a normal course," she said with dismay. "If that is the way he treats a woman he's only just met, imagine what he has in store for the one who is legally bound to honor and obey him."

A twitch in his jaw let her know her point struck home. He didn't respond with his usual verbal parry and his expression hinted he was more affected than he revealed. Was it too much to hope that he might have second thoughts about inflicting a husband on her?

She watched him test his right hand, flex it and wince. Her breath caught in her throat. His knuckles were swelling.

He had defended her.

She relived in her mind's eye the moment when he'd slammed into Clapford to keep him from reaching her…the way his big frame braced and strained…the fierce determination in his face. The elemental female in her savored the raw male power that had come to her defense. The rational woman in her wanted to express how grateful she was. But the feminine heart of her wanted to curl up around that battered hand and soothe—

A well-timed shiver claimed the rest of that thought. She forced her gaze away from him, and it fell on her cold, sodden footwear.

"My shoes." She hiked her skirt to the top of her nine-button boot. "I didn't realize I'd stepped into the water. They're wet through and through."

Mercy bent to feel the leather. "We got to get ye out o' them, miz." She patted the seat beside her, then reached into her carpet bag for a button hook. "Set yer feet up here. We'll get ye warmed right up."

Jack jerked his chin back. "We?"

# 10

"BREAK OUT yer flask, sarr," Mercy ordered, glowering when he hesitated. "She needs a nip. And don't pretend ye ain't got one. Genl'men always got a drop tucked away somewhere."

His jaw loosened at the old girl's audacity, but he reached into a compartment under the seat and retrieved a silver flask. Removing the cap, he took a sizeable swallow himself before passing it over to Mercy, who astounded him by doing the same before handing it off to Mariah.

"This is outrageous," he said, his eyes narrowing on the trim ankles and French-heeled boots now on the seat. He could barely swallow.

"Removing my cold, wet shoes to prevent catching pneumonia is outrageous?" Mariah took a drink from the flask and closed her eyes, clearly appreciating its warmth. "I suppose you think a lady should rather die from lung sickness than reveal her ankles?"

*Hell, yes,* he wanted to say. He managed to rise above it.

"Then, it's a good thing that I'm a simple widowed innkeeper instead of a lady." She sank back, cradling the flask against her breasts. "Absurd, isn't it, how society decides such things? A woman in a ball gown bares her entire bosom with impunity, but let a man catch a glimpse of a common, ordinary ankle—"

"I think you've had quite enough brandy," he said, holding out a hand for the flask. She ignored it.

"All the more nonsensical because ankles aren't erotically responsive and breasts are," she continued. "However did such a paradox come to be?" When Mercy's surprise turned into a frown, she winked at the old girl and took another sip. "Speaking philosophically, of course. Every topic is allowed in discourse on natural and social philosophy. Is that not so, Jack?"

"Pay her no mind, sarr—she jus' likes to talk hot peppers," Mercy said, scowling at her mistress. "She were alwus tormentin' the old squire."

"Teasing," she corrected. "And he liked it."

Mercy addressed Jack. "He let her get by wi' a lot, sarr."

Mariah affirmed that comment with a mischievous smile. "Because I let *him* get by with a lot."

Jack could barely follow the exchange; he was stuck on *erotically responsive.* The words had set his blood humming and his skin aching. That sin-tainted smile…she was determined to provoke him and he was just as determined not to allow himself to be provoked. Not in that way.

Not again. Too damned much was at stake.

To think that moments ago he was thinking of her as selfless and upright and telling himself she deserved better than Bertie's wandering lust.

Mercy inspected the boot and set it on the floor to dry. "Yer stockin's soaked clear through." She shook her head. "Better take it off, too, miz."

Mariah lifted her knee and reached beneath her skirt to undo her garter and slide the stocking down her leg. It was all Jack could do to keep his tongue in his mouth as the maid draped the stocking over the seat beside him. The knitted silk retained the erotically charged shape of her leg.

"That feels wonderful." Mariah closed her eyes as Mercy rubbed her foot briskly with the blanket and started on the other shoe. She wiggled her toes under the cover. "Much better."

For a long, harrowing moment, he was unable to tear his gaze from the suggestive bump her toes made under that cover. Then he mustered the will to tilt his hat over his eyes and jam his shoulders back into the seat.

SOMETIME LATER, Mariah awakened feeling a little cramped but deliciously warm. Her head and shoulder were propped against the side of the coach and her feet were drawn up beneath her skirts on the seat. As she pushed upright, she smelled sandalwood and soap and "essence of Jack." Looking down, she found a familiar charcoal-gray suit coat spread over her, its sleeves tucked around her. She felt a rush of pleasure. It was as if the coat was proxy for the arms of its owner…who sat across from her in his waistcoat and shirtsleeves…watching her.

The rosy light of sunset cast a dusky glow over his angular face and lent a sheen to his bronze eyes. She tried not to stare. Or want. And failed.

"Are we almost there?" she asked, her throat tight.

"At the outskirts of Cambridge."

"About time." She pushed upright, conscious of the location of every part of her body in relation to his. "I am desperate to stretch my legs."

He consulted his watch, holding it up into a wedge of bright light coming through the window. "We'll have a bit of supper while I make inquiries. I still have connections among the faculty, but I doubt we'll locate Martindale before tomorrow." He sounded distracted. "There is an excellent hotel—the University Arms—overlooking Parker's Piece in the center of the city. We should be able to find rooms there."

"A warm meal and a clean, comfortable bed." She smoothed wrinkles from his coat as it lay over her lap. "I never fully appreciated how important they are to travelers. This gives me a new perspective on my own inn."

He took a deep breath and fixed his gaze on the wall behind her.

"Mrs. Eller—"

"Mariah, please." She sensed something important was coming.

"Mariah," he said, as if it were a hurdle he had to jump. "I want you to know that I am not insensible to your situation. I know now that this liaison with the prince was not your idea. And I recognize that this marriage requirement has lasting consequences for you. It may not be how you wanted to spend your life, but…it is my hope that we can find someone who will be genuinely acceptable to you as a husband."

"That is very thoughtful of you," she said, relaxing as warmth toward him bloomed in her core and flowed into her smile.

"It only makes sense." He tensed sharply and looked away. "After all, if you are unhappy, you won't be a very good 'friend' to the prince."

She felt as if he'd just tossed icy pond water on her. Every time she thought she glimpsed some humanity, some warmth or sincerity in him… She yanked his coat from her and tossed it into a heap on the seat beside him.

"Are you sure you want me to be a good 'friend' to the prince, Jack?" She speared him with a look that her husband had always likened to blue Damascus steel. "Perhaps you'd rather I be *your* 'friend' instead."

Even in the darkening coach she could see she'd struck sparks.

"You know, while your esteemed husband was *educating* you," he said irritably, "he might have found time to teach you a bit of discretion. Along with some propriety and sense of a woman's place in the world."

She leaned over to snatch up her stockings and boots.

"Sorry. Didn't have time. He was too busy teaching me thirty-seven different ways to make a man moan." She turned sideways on the seat and folded her skirt and petticoats back.

Lifting one bare leg, she slid toes into the stocking and slowly—*ever so slowly*—pulled it up while raising her leg. A leg he had explored so briefly but memorably in her hotel room yesterday. When the silk stocking was smoothed up her calf and over her knee, she slipped the garter on and rolled it into place. Halfway through the second stocking, there it was: a quiet, tormented exhalation. She aimed her smile straight ahead, while glancing at him from the corner of her eye.

"That," she said with a purr, "was number nine."

THE NARROW Cambridge streets were crowded with black-robed students emptying out of libraries, lecture halls and tutors' offices into the town's taverns. The coach had to stop periodically to wait for the throngs of boisterous students to clear. Jack commented that the wheels of Cambridge scholarship—like those of academia everywhere—were lubricated by the nectars of grape and grain. He knew that, he revealed, because some years earlier he had been one of those parched Cambridge scholars headed for the closest tavern at the end of the day.

The gas streetlamps had been lit by the time they reached the University Arms in the center of the city. The large, Gothic-style hotel was furnished with all the modern conveniences: a number of bathing rooms *en suite*, a ladies' sitting room, a library and a well-regarded restaurant that served dinner into the evening. After freshening up in their rooms, Mariah and Mercy met Jack downstairs for dinner.

The dining room was large and appointed with fine linen, crystal and china that reminded Mariah of her childhood home. As Jack explained that he had sent inquiries about Winston

Martindale to old acquaintances and was awaiting word, she ran her hands over the silver and rolled her empty wineglass back and forth, watching the light reflected in its facets.

It had been a long time since she had thought of her girlhood home…of the way her lovely mother always dressed for dinner and how dignified her father had looked in his evening clothes. They had insisted Mariah take meals with them in the dining room instead of in the nursery, even when they entertained. They were determined that, despite being an only child, she would have a strong sense of family. The thought gave her a hollow feeling. *Family.* Once she had dreamed of having a home and children—

"Are you listening?" Jack asked with annoyance.

"Sorry." She abandoned the stemmed glass on the tabletop and smoothed her napkin across her lap. "You were saying?"

He had just begun to repeat his plan for the next day when a stout-looking older man with a ruddy complexion and pro-digious mutton chops appeared in the arched entrance to the dining room.

"There you are, my boy!"

At the sound of that voice, Jack was on his feet and turning with an outstretched hand and a huge smile.

"Professor Jamison! How good to see you. You didn't have to come here, sir. I intended to call on you first thing tomorrow morning."

"Balderdash. Did you think I wouldn't hurry across campus to see my favorite student, no matter what the hour?" He pumped Jack's hand as he clapped him affectionately on the shoulder. Jack basked in his professor's delight until the old boy's gaze fell on Mariah. "Well, well, St. Lawrence." Jamison's grin broadened. "I hadn't heard that you had married."

"Married? *No!*" Jack said too loudly, then reddened. "May I present Mrs. Mariah Eller. We've come to Cambridge to, um—"

"Locate a gentleman. On a legal matter," Mariah provided. "Pleased to meet you, professor."

"Charmed, Mrs. Eller." Jamison made a courtly bow over her extended hand and then nodded politely to Mercy, whose single-name introduction and simple garments indicated her role as lady's companion.

"Won't you join us for dinner?" Mariah waved to the unused fourth place at their table.

"With pleasure." He quickly took a seat. "St. Lawrence, I never thought to find you in the company of ladies." He raised his eyebrows and leaned toward Mariah. "Not 'Iron Jack.' All work and no play—that was his motto. Never met a more serious eighteen-year-old in my life."

With that, his garrulous mentor began to recount tales of Jack's student days that made Jack wince and look pained. The professor, undaunted by his former student's chagrin and encouraged by Mariah's interest, rambled on to draw a portrait of an eager and driven young man.

"Rewrote the answers to his exams after scores were assigned. Checked and rechecked his measurements and calculations. Was twice the scholar his brothers were. Would have made a superb scientist. Mathematics came as natural as breathing for him. Damned fine mind." Jamison sighed, wagging his head. "Begged him to stay on, you know. Had a number of projects for him to undertake as graduate studies. But it was not to be. The faculty still laments his loss to the bright lights and fast company of London."

"A man has obligations, Professor," Jack said uncomfortably, studying the wine in his glass.

"To his country, of course. To his family, unquestionably."

Jamison spoke in a way that made it clear they had discussed this point before. "But also to *himself*." The professor studied him with visible regret. "One must endeavor to see that all three are served by the course one chooses in life. To neglect to use one's talents and opportunities is to deny Destiny. And Destiny has a way of calling us to account for unused gifts."

Mariah noted the way Jack's face tightened and saw in him traces of the young boy he had been: full of promise and torn between conflicting goals. And there were those *brothers* of his again. She warmed to the recurring image of him as the always-pushed, ever-hungry "third of five."

When Jack caught her watching him with a discerning gaze, he cleared his throat to change the subject.

"Back to the business that brought us here. What about this Winston Martindale? Do you know him, Professor?"

"As it happens, I do. He is another old student of mine. Before your time. Don't get me wrong, he's a decent enough chap. Now a fellow in Philosophy at Magdalene College. But hardly a serious scholar. Does most of his 'supervisions' of an evening—" he paused "—at the Quill and Scroll."

Jack sat back with a look of distaste. "Thank you, Professor. I shall try to catch Martindale someplace more conducive to a lady's business."

"What is this Quill and Scroll?" Mariah studied Jack's disapproval.

"An ale house frequented by students," the professor provided.

"What's a perfessor doin' overseein' a tavern?" Mercy asked.

"Not that kind of supervision," Jack explained. "Supervisions here at Cambridge are the core of the teaching-learning process. The fellows hold individual or small-group tutorials in which students discuss their studies, present their work and are evaluated. And Martindale…"

"Conducts his in an ale house," Mariah said when he paused. It didn't speak well for her prospective husband.

When dinner was over and the professor had departed and they headed upstairs, Mariah spotted Jack collecting his hat and coat from his room and trying to slip past her.

"Where are you going at this hour?" She planted herself in his path.

He fingered the brim of his hat and refused to meet her gaze.

"You're going to this Quill and Scroll, aren't you?" She read her answer in his avoidance. "Well, not without me, you aren't."

"Look, I know this place," he said, exasperated. "The Quill and Scroll is an old college hall that was bought by a German brew master and turned into a large tavern. It's loud, rude and not at all suitable for ladies."

Was this new designation as a "lady" an elevation or a dismissal?

"All the more reason I should accompany you. I need to see my prospects in their natural settings, whether appropriate for ladies or not." She turned to Mercy. "Don't let him leave without me."

The loyal maid positioned herself between Jack and the stairs, crossed her ample arms and glowered. Shortly, Mariah returned, wearing her coat and hat, and gave the old woman a one-armed hug.

"You needn't wait up, Mercy. After such a long day, I'm sure you're exhausted."

Mercy nodded gratefully.

"Careful, miz. Them students look none too trusty."

# *11*

THAT WAS how she and Jack came to be entering the noisy hall of the Quill and Scroll at ten o'clock on a weekday evening. The place was filled with smoke, the scent of spilled ale and tables ringed by a motley collection of chairs and benches swiped from lecture halls. Generations of aspiring scholars had whiled away their undergraduate years on those worn seats and carved their names for posterity in the posts and beams that held up the roof.

All the way over in the cab, Jack had admonished her to stay close, let him do the talking and not engage any of the drunken students. He behaved as if she—essentially a tavern-keeper herself—had never been in an ale house before. By the time he steered her briskly to the crowded bar to inquire after Winston Martindale, she was roundly annoyed.

They were directed to one side of a massive fireplace, where two groups of young men in black robes were engaged in a rowdy and freewheeling dispute. As she and Jack approached, it became clear that their discourse was being refereed by a portly, red-faced fellow in a scholar's robe and cap. He had on the table before him a stand holding a line of wooden beads, which he shuttled back and forth with sausage-like digits whenever one of the sides made a point. *Martindale.*

Oh, dear.

They watched for a few minutes, trying to make sense of

the ale-fueled chaos. Between issuing "hear-hear's" and awarding points in the debate, the pudgy professor gnawed on a roast turkey leg and sucked ale from a large tankard. Then he caught sight of Mariah watching him.

"Whoa-ho—we have company, ladsss!" he roared. "Mind your mannersss and make some room!" He shoved to his feet and beckoned. "Come, join usss, my lovely. And you, too—" he pointed at Jack with his drumstick "—whoever you are. Beer—get our visitors sssome beer!"

"Jack St. Lawrence, Professor Martindale. And this is Mrs. Eller." Jack held his top hat with one hand and Mariah's elbow with the other. He looked over the seats the students had vacated and urged Mariah forward. "We were hoping we might have a private word with you."

A wave of *oooh*'s from the students and calls of "Winnie needs a word with a lai-dy!" mingled with derisive laughter and drunken male giggles. Winston ordered the students away, calling them ingrates and sophomoric twits and pelting them with crusts of bread. When the three were finally seated together at the ale-sticky table, Martindale wiped his greasy hands on his robe and looked Mariah over…a bit too appreciatively.

"Now what's ssso urgent that it must interrupt my sssupervisionsss?"

That was when she noticed how odd the professor's teeth were. Huge and unnaturally white…all exactly the same shape…like the staves of a picket fence. When his grin broadened, she saw that his gums were gray and realized that they—like his enormous teeth—were artificial. Which accounted for the mushy nature of his *s*'s.

"I never object to being interrupted by one of the Gracesss," he said, reaching for her hand with smarmy familiarity. "Essspecially Beauty."

"We are putting together a roster of speakers—" Mariah scrambled to concoct a story as she freed herself from his grasp "—for a lecture tour, and hope to include a professor who can address advances in modern knowledge. The topic of our tour will be 'The Future: Are There Any Mysteries Left?' We were given your name and hope to add you to our list of speakers."

"Given my name?" He seemed delighted at first, but pleasure soon gave way to confusion. "By whom?"

Mariah turned to Jack, but he gave her a don't-look-at-me-this-is-your-story scowl, and she answered with the name closest to her tongue.

"The Prince of Wales."

"The Prince of—you got my name from *the Prince of Wales?* For a lissst of ssspeakersss?" He shook off some of his bleariness. Looking from Mariah to Jack and back, he was struck by a tardy burst of comprehension.

"But that's not the lissst you truly mean, isss it? I'm on the *lissst* again!" He clapped his hands as a schoolboy does at the prospect of licorice whips. "They've put me back on the husssband lissst." Then he astonished both Mariah and Jack by fixing her with a conspiratorial grin.

"Is it you?" he said with a giggle, barely able to keep himself in his chair. "Jenkies—you're a beauty, my girl. You could do better than me."

"What?" Mariah jerked back on the bench, grabbing Jack's arm to steady herself. "What are you talking about?"

"They've put me back on the lissst to marry one of the prince'sss lady friends, right?" He looked around, as if trying out the notion in his head. "Usssed to be tried out quite regular. Thought those dayssss were over." He jiggled with excitement. "Mussst 'ave heard about my new teeth." He turned his head from side to side, grinning like a Cheshire cat to show them off. "Imported, you know. From Germany. Quite the clever little craftsssmen, those Hunsss."

To impress her further, he took them out—uppers and lowers—and put them on the table for her to admire.

She stared at that set of huge porcelain teeth with bits of turkey caught between them and clapped a hand over her mouth.

Jack was on his feet in a heartbeat and pulling her up. She was aware of him telling Martindale that he was sadly mistaken and that they would find someone else for their "lecture tour," before ushering her out.

She was still seeing big porcelain-white teeth before her eyes when they reached the pavement outside.

"I told you it was no place for a lady," he said in a choked voice as he propelled her along. "You should have listened and stayed at the hotel."

"And miss seeing that?" She found her voice. "Not for all the tea in China." The full impact of it hit her. "He just popped his teeth out of his head!" She stopped on the pavement, pantomimed him plopping them on the table in front her, and then burst into giggles of disbelief. "Lord—I thought he was going to insist I try them out! Can you imagine?" She bared her teeth, feigning she was bucktoothed, and clacked her uppers and lowers together…before dissolving into full gales of laughter.

RELIEF ALLOWED Jack to chuckle at her expression. Then an internal barrier snapped and he joined her in shoulder-quaking laughs; the sort that dispel tension and remind people of their common ground in humor.

He hadn't laughed like this in—well, in a very long time.

Weakened, she leaned against him. It seemed only natural to put an arm around her in support, and for the next few moments he gave himself over to the pleasure that migrated into him through that contact. His blood warmed as something new and precious unfolded around his heart.

Her eyes shimmered with moisture as she looked up, and he reached into his breast pocket, intending to offer her his handkerchief. Instead, he found himself dabbing her eyes. His other hand came up to cup her warm cheek and he stared down into dark-centered blue pools filled with genuine pleasure. A surge of protectiveness washed over him.

"Did you really get his name from the earl of Chester?" she asked.

He nodded, grappling with the strength of this new feeling.

"Though, I believe he did say it was his son's recommendation." He looked back at the doors of the Quill and Scroll. "The little sod. Probably had a good laugh handing over the name of his toothless old tutor."

"Well, I had a good laugh, too, so I won't hold it against him. Or against you. Though, I confess, I am losing all faith in this list of yours."

"I had no idea, Mariah," he said. "I was asked to solicit names from among the prince's intimates and I...trusted their judgment."

She winced as if she were about to confess a mortal sin.

"Heaven help me, I believe you."

He offered her his arm as they began to walk and he set a leisurely pace that seemed perfect for the cool autumn night. Together they wound their way in companionable silence along the cobblestone streets beneath gas lamps that cast circles of soft golden light.

"That's three out of four," she said, pulling him back to the reality of yet another failed husband prospect.

"Three out of bloody four," he echoed.

"So, what happens if I fail to marry in the next eleven days?"

He felt his gut tense and mouth dry in spite of himself.

"There is still one name on the list," he said. Not that he expected the last candidate to be much different from the others. Not that he *wanted* that candidate to be different. He felt a peculiar weight against his chest and sent a hand to the envelope in his inner pocket. The damned license never let him forget for a minute that she was meant for someone else.

"Why should I believe he will be any more suitable? One was spoken for. Another was a mean-spirited bully." She displayed the count on her fingers. "And the third was a feckless little squab with deplorable dental hygiene. I could do better standing in a town square yelling for volunteers."

"You can't cry off—I've already paid your blessed mortgage."

"I didn't say I was crying off. I just think it's time for a different approach, that's all. If I'm to be married within eleven days, I need to find more suitable husband candidates." They had to pause to avoid a group of well-oiled students staggering out of a pub and stumbling arm-in-arm down the middle of the street. "That means going where men of substance and ambition gather." She pulled him to a halt, searching some mental image. "I should go straight to London and search for my own husband."

London. He groaned. He had hoped to leave it to her future husband to take her there and escort her through the appointments with dressmakers and milliners and visits to linen drapers and haberdashers. Now he was not only going to have to help her shop for gloves and corsets and stockings, he was going to have to help her shop for a man!

"And just how do you plan to carry on this search?" he said, annoyance rising to ruin his mood.

"In a perfectly logical and organized fashion," she said, raising her chin and striking off briskly in the direction of their hotel. "I'm going to make a *list*."

# 12

"WHAT THE DEVIL do you think you are doing?" Jack demanded in a loud whisper as Mariah pulled him down the third-floor hallway—past his hotel room and toward hers. "It's almost midnight." He gestured to the gaslights that had been extinguished everywhere but the lobby and stairwells. "You saw the look the desk clerk gave us when I asked for our room keys."

"His depraved imaginings are *his* problem," she said, unlocking her door and pulling him inside with her. He stood as stiff as a pole, holding his room key in a death grip, while she closed the door and lit the lamp.

"A lady doesn't entertain gentlemen in her room at this late—"

"I'm not a lady, remember? I'm a widow who is about to become a 'wife of convenience' and a prince's mistress." She adjusted the lamp wick so that the room was softly lit, and she swayed toward him as she removed her gloves and let her coat slide down her shoulders. "But how sweet of you to say you find me 'entertaining.'"

He felt a stir of anticipation in his loins and scowled.

"I don't believe I said that."

"I've noticed you don't believe a lot of the things you say."

While he sorted out that comment, she pulled his hat from his hands and replaced it with a pad of paper and a pen taken from her trunk.

"What is this?" He held the writing materials by two fingers, as if they were strange artifacts of an unknown civilization.

"Sit." She pointed to the lone upholstered chair. "And make notes."

"I beg your pardon. I am not a clerk," he said defensively. "And I refuse to participate in whatever deviousness you have in mind. It has nothing to do with me."

"It has everything to do with you." She removed her hat and jacket, then pulled the overstuffed chair closer to the coal-burning hearth and gave the seat a pat, ordering him to sit. "Once I find a man who meets my requirements, you will have to convince him to cooperate and wed me."

"I can't imagine that would be necessary." He eyed the seat with a tightening in his belly. "You're quite persuasive enough on your own."

"You'd think so, wouldn't you?" She pushed him over to the chair, opened his greatcoat, and pulled it down his shoulders. "But men can be appallingly stubborn. *Sit.*"

He perched on the edge of the chair, pitched like Chinese fireworks ready to launch, and watched her hang his coat on a hook by the door. Her movements were fluid and unself-conscious, almost…hypnotic.

He shook himself more alert.

"Where to start?" She paced a few steps away and traced her lip thoughtfully. "Tall. Definitely. Somewhere near your height. With a manly frame and bearing." She smiled as her gaze drifted over him.

"What the devil are you doing?"

"Making a list of things I want in a husband. Muscles. I do like muscles on a man. Not the hammer-wielding-black-smith or beefy-field-hand sort. More the rowing-archery-expert-horsemanship kind." She startled him by taking hold of his arm—"You don't mind, do you?"—and feeling it up and down. She lingered with a pleased expression over his tensed and bulging bicep. "Muscles very like yours, in fact."

As she released him, his arm ached from greatly increased blood flow. That vigorous circulation spread through the rest of him, causing pressure in body parts that were going to get him in trouble if he stayed much longer.

"And let's not forget good teeth," she said with a wicked chuckle. "Nothing worse than having to kiss a man with rotten or missing teeth." She made her buck-toothed face again, drawing a startled laugh from him. Then she pulled his gaze into hers, eyes twinkling, and bit that luscious lower lip of hers. "And you know how fond I am of kissing."

She was wrong earlier, he thought, watching her resume pacing up and down the room. There wasn't a man in Britain who could resist her when she was determined to be irresistible. As she was now.

"As for hair, I'm not fussy. Any color, as long as it's plentiful." As she passed, she reached over to rake her fingers through his dark waves. His scalp tingled and every hair on his body came to attention. "And soft. I love the contrast between soft hair and hard muscles. And I do love to curl my fingers in a man's hair when I—" She gave an exaggerated shiver. "Are you getting all of this down?"

She moved to peer over his shoulder at the empty pad in his hands.

"Oh. No wonder you're having trouble writing." Her voice lowered as she slid around him in such a way that she pressed against him the whole time. "You still have your gloves on."

Standing before him, she seized his hands and *bit* the kidskin at the end of one finger, tugging it with her teeth. The pad and pen he held tumbled to the floor as his whole body went rigid. One by one, she bit the tips of his glove fingers and slowly, with provocative leisure, drew them off. By the time she reached for his other hand, his body was as taut as a bass string and vibrating with arousal. Then she raised his naked hand and nibbled the pads of his fingers with those perfect teeth and ripe lips.

He clenched his jaw and his indrawn breath turned into a hiss.

This was nothing short of torture.

What had he done to deserve this? He had kept the prince's hunting revelries within bounds and seen to it that Bertie always made it to his bed and…*usurped the prince's enjoyment of a woman he had clearly intended to bed.*

That sobering thought threw him one last lifeline of sanity.

"I can't do this." His voice was an octave lower as he dragged his tingling hand back and pushed to his feet. She didn't give an inch; he had to make room to stand by forcing the chair back with his legs. On his feet but badly off balance, he had to fight the pull of those forget-me-not-blue eyes.

"On the contrary." She shifted, brushing against the bulge in his trousers with knee-weakening accuracy. "You seem quite capable."

He groaned. "Don't do this, Mariah."

"Don't do what?" The humor in her face gave way to a compelling earnestness. "Respond like a woman instead of a commodity? Don't presume to take pleasure and passion where I can? Don't try to steal a bit of joy and companionship before I go into a harness of carnal obligation?"

*Pleasure, joy, companionship;* each word struck like a chisel, engraving itself on his heart. But it was the word *steal* that proved sharp enough to pierce his conscience.

"You belong to the prince," he said thickly.

"Not yet, I don't. Until I marry and go to the prince's bed, I belong to no one but myself."

She slipped her hands around his collar, pulling his head

down so that his mouth hovered above hers, so that warm breath and the incidental brush of lips against lips added to the persuasion of her words.

"In eleven days I'll be married again, and indentured to the bed of a prince who values his carnal pleasures above my feelings, my personal worth and my freedom. But right now if I choose to share my bed and body, that is my decision and mine alone."

She was right; the prince neither knew nor wanted to know about her distaste for what he required of her. That acknowledgment went straight to his core, illuminating the shameful fact that his abstinence was not inspired by true virtue or in consideration of his patron prince. Rather, it was but a tool of his own ambition. His self-denial was both self-serving and a sham.

"Just once, before I go into that miserable servitude, I want to make love because *I* desire it. Not because I am coerced or because it is a marital duty or even because it is the prudent thing to do. I want to make love for the pure joy and pleasure of it." She ran her hand tenderly down his cheek. "And I want to do it with someone I like very much."

*She liked him.*

When she stretched up to press her mouth against his, he'd have had to be made of hammered steel to resist kissing her back. And despite what his old tutor had said, he was not made of anything half so incorruptible. He did, however, manage to resist pulling her against him…

…until she ran her tongue between his lips with such deliberate provocation that he felt as if he had just been dropped into a blast furnace. Heat enveloped him; his arms enveloped her; and a heartbeat later they were as close as paper and sealing wax.

He trembled with the need to plunge his hands into her warm-honey hair and pull it loose, to bury his face in it and rub it all over his bare chest and naked body. He ran his hands feverishly over her, seeking out every line, texture and curve he had mentally claimed in the last three days. Images of stockings and bare ankles and the tactile memory of naked thighs made his skin come alive with a hunger for that same kind of stimulation.

More. He wanted *more*.

When she broke off that stream of kisses, he was mildly shocked to find his bones felt as if they wouldn't support weight or movement. As he scrambled to recoup, she grabbed his hand and pulled him toward the bed.

EVERY PARTICLE of her body was vibrating with need. But not a garden variety, take-a-brandy-and-it-will-pass kind of urge. This was a bone-deep, part-of-me-is-missing kind of feeling…a hunger that reached all the way down into the soul and stretched and shoved and rearranged inner furnishings until it made room for something life-changing.

More. She wanted *more*.

She wanted to feel his weight bearing down on her, his heat searing her flesh, his passion filling her until she couldn't breathe or think.

With her blood singing in her ears, she trapped his gaze in hers and began to work the buttons of her blouse. The starched cotton slid down her bare arms and dropped to the floor. Her belt and skirt went next, falling into a dark pool at her feet. She stood in petticoats and corset, sensing his hunger and praying desire would exert its inscrutable force.

"I'm offering, Jack," she said, her heart thudding as she reached up to remove several pins and let her hair tumble over her shoulders. He seemed to have turned to stone, standing there, watching her as she ran her fingers through her hair and let it fall into a hedonistic tangle.

"Enjoy me. Let me enjoy you. Before it's too late."

With a muffled moan, he bore her back onto the bed and sank onto the soft mattress over her.

Electricity arced along her nerves, unleashing desire, making every movement, every action a rebellious celebration of freedom. She wrapped her arms around his neck and opened to his penetrating kisses as she arched and pressed her breasts against him, urging him to release her.

Moments later her laces were free and she lay in a tangle of half-shed garments, beckoning him to a sensory banquet. He rubbed his face in her light hair and inhaled, murmuring his findings.

"You smell like heliotrope—" he breathed her in "—and jasmine and honey. Damn me if you don't smell downright *edible.*"

She gave a throaty laugh as he ripped off his coat and vest and flung them aside. With trembling hands, he peeled away her chemise.

Her breath caught as he buried his face between her breasts and rubbed his hot face over her cool skin. As his kisses and caresses trailed down her body, pleasure radiated into every curve and crevice. Soon he was grazing her with his teeth and she felt a drawing sensation in her sex that started a familiar chain of responses.

Her body tensed, her lips swelled, her pupils dilated and her sex began to burn with a thick, slow-swirling flame. Trembling with escalating pleasure, she directed his mouth over her shoulders and breasts until he reached her nipple and tongued and sucked that pebble-hard flesh.

When she couldn't stand the longing anymore, she pushed him up and reached for his shirt buttons.

"Clothes…now…off," she said, barely able to string words together. "Feel…all…you…over…"

A minute later, his shirt was gone and his chest descended on her like a living wall, crushing her breasts, giving her the weight and pressure she wanted. Air escaped her on a ragged moan. She raked his bare back with her fingernails and savored the way he responded with deeper, harder kisses.

As he ran his hands up the insides of her legs, she parted them and raised her stocking-clad legs on either side of him, wanting to wrap them around him. Then his fingers found her hot, wet core and she shivered, startled by the intensity of the sensation. His hand was firm but gentle as he read her reactions and adjusted his touch.

Time seemed to stop as he toyed deliberately with her, tracing lazy circles on her slick, heated flesh, bringing her to the edge of climax. She moaned with both pleasure and need, pressing against his hand, seeking a deeper, more satisfying contact. When his fingers slipped inside her, she tightened around them, relishing the rush of pleasure it released.

Gripping his back, she rode mounting waves of excitation, rising, expanding, then crashing through sensory boundaries into pure pleasure.

For a moment she couldn't see or feel, could only float within a steamy cloud of mingled presence. When she opened her eyes it was to a pair of molten bronze disks, glowing with appreciation and desire.

"You do have the touch, Jack B. Nimble," she whispered, pressing against him, more energized than sated. "Let's see what else you have."

She pushed him back and sat up, abandoning her garments as she rolled him onto his back. Straddling him, she swept her hair across his bare chest and laughed at the way he sucked air. She dragged her breasts up the midline of his body then she reversed course and retraced that path.

He twitched, tensed and then relaxed into a groan of

pleasure. When she reached his trouser buttons, he grabbed her hands.

"You don't have to," he said hoarsely.

"Don't have to?" She registered the anxiety that had entered his expression. "I want to give pleasure as well as receive it, remember?"

The look in his eyes as he released her made her pause for a moment. Did he not believe her? Not trust her? For a moment she wondered what kind of sexual experiences had led him to impose such limits.

"You make me feel alive, Jack. And wanted." She stuffed every bit of her longing and gratitude into a smile and aimed it straight for his heart. "I want to do the same for you."

This time when she worked the buttons of his trousers, he didn't object, but she felt him go taut as she slid down and rubbed her face against the still-covered ridge of his erection. He gasped as she caressed him through the fabric and then slowly nudged his trousers aside.

She ogled, eyes widening.

"That is truly a thing of beauty, Jack." She dispelled his anxiety with a beaming smile. "Remind me to put one of those on my list."

# 13

It TOOK a second to register. His jaw dropped. Then he caught the mischief in her grin and pulled her up so she was face to face with him.

"You and your damnable list. Don't think I haven't noticed you making me the prototype for your future husband. I conveniently seem to have everything you've mentioned, thus far."

"So you *did* notice," she said with a wicked edge. "I was beginning to think you were a little thick, Jack. And not where it counts." She bent her knee and drew her leg up his body, sliding it pointedly over his erection.

He laughed in spite of himself and seemed a little shocked to find himself doing so.

"You're a jade, you know that?"

"A circumspect and socially appropriate jade," she corrected, giving him a look that was half virtue, half vice and wholly unrepentant. "I was trained by a master. My well-traveled squire could have taught Sir Richard Burton and his *Kama Sutra* a thing or two."

His jaw loosened again.

"The *Kama*—y-you know about that?" His surprise deepened at the glint of knowledge in her eyes. "You've seen it?"

"Seen it, read it and improved on it." She giggled at the shock on his face. "Want me to show you one of my favorites?"

He looked uncertain at first, then—pride at stake—made himself nod.

"Just lie back…close your eyes…and open your senses," she ordered, smiling. When he obeyed, she put her face near his and fluttered her eyelashes so that they tickled his cheek. She paused for a moment, then did the same on the other side. Covering his face with quick sweeps of her long lashes, she ended at his lips, which parted as she brushed them with flirtatious strokes.

His eyes opened to reveal a tangle of potent emotions.

"Did you feel it?" she said, afraid he might have been disappointed.

He nodded and whispered, "What was that?"

She studied his surprise.

"You honestly didn't peek, did you?"

Warmth cascaded through her as he shook his head. Honorable Jack. She bit her lip and bent to flutter her eyelashes against his cheek and then his lips. He was so still, she could feel him absorbing every stroke, drinking in every nuance. By the time she moved away, he was holding his breath.

"It's called 'The Butterfly.'" She smiled, feeling strangely exposed in expressing so girlish a preference. "Appreciating it requires an inner quietness and an openness to simple pleasures. Proof that you don't have to make the earth tremble in order to give another physical delight."

His eyes were heating, his breath coming faster.

"Of course—" she braced, unable to read what was happening in him "—earth-quaking is good, too. I mean, each certainly has its place."

A moment later he had rolled her beneath him and was kissing her witless.

"Wait," she gasped out between kisses, "I didn't get to—ohhh—"

Those agile hands of his were busy again and this time they had help. He slid between her thighs and she felt his shaft settling into the cleft of her sex and starting to move. It was lovely. Heart-stoppingly gorgeous, in fact. Long, rhythmic slides that increased in pressure and friction and quickly pushed her to the edge of climax again.

She tilted her pelvis and felt his sex poised to enter her. When she tried to urged him inside, he stiffened and held himself back.

"Are you sure?" he whispered, trembling.

Smiling, she tightened her legs around him and clasped him harder against her. She slipped her hands into his hair and used it to pull his mouth to hers…as he slid inside her…inch by steamy, voluptuous inch. By the time he lay fully imbedded in her, she could scarcely breathe. He was so hot and full and thick. She could feel his pulse drumming inside her.

Closing her eyes, she gave herself over to the pleasure of that steamy completion. He filled her in a way that left no part of her untouched. It was so different than her former experiences; so much more intimate and overwhelming, so much more pleasurable on every level.

When he started to move, she absorbed his thrusts and slowly gave up control. Taking him in deeper, she met his motion, seeking harder contact and greater friction. Intensity mounted until she couldn't absorb another single sensation and her overstuffed senses shattered.

In the midst of that explosion, she felt him withdraw and take his release between them. It took a few moments for her senses to clear and for her to realize he'd done so to protect her from *consequences*. A brief pang of loss was quickly replaced by understanding, then gratitude. Even in the grip of passion, his ingrained sense of responsibility hadn't failed him.

When he slid to the bed beside her and pulled her against him, she curled into him, entwining her legs with his. It felt strangely as if they were still joined. Then he smiled down at her, and his warm golden eyes and sexy, just-for-you smile made her heart forget to beat.

"Are you all right?" he asked, brushing her hair back.

"Better than all right." She dropped a kiss on his chest and slid her arm across his waist. "I've never felt like sesame seeds before."

"What?" His chuckle rumbled beneath her ear.

"Another little gem from the *Kama Sutra*." She smiled. "When lovers entwine such that they forget where one ends and the other begins, they are said to have blended like 'sesame seeds and rice.'"

"So, I am *rice?*" He sounded confused, but when she looked up he was grinning.

"Tonight, you're the rice—" she just managed to keep from using the possessive *my* rice "—to my sesame seeds."

He studied her face, gave a wry nod, then lifted her chin to give her an achingly gentle kiss.

Sometime later she roused from drowsiness to the feel of his big body hardening against her. She stretched luxuriously, rubbing her breasts against his side and stomach, knowing full well the invitation she was sending. His eyes took on a glint of arousal as he rolled her onto her back.

"Your husband taught you all of this?" he asked, nuzzling her neck.

"He did."

"And you were how old when he began this 'tutoring'?"

"Old enough to be mortified. Young enough to get over it."

"And still you speak well of him."

"You have to understand—he was careful with me." She made him stop kissing her shoulder and look at her. "He made me comfortable and never asked me to do anything I didn't want to do. He was a very wise man, Mason Eller. He introduced me to my own desires and then let them lead me on a path of exploration."

"Which he enjoyed as much as you did," he concluded.

"Of course. He wasn't a hypocrite. He never pretended to do it solely for my benefit. But that's the way of things in a marriage. You give of yourself…your care, effort and passion…trusting that the same will be returned to you. In a good marriage, it always is."

"So, you honestly believe yours was a good marriage?"

"I do. It wasn't a grand romance, but it was loving. And even fun at times. He showed me that laughter and passion make great partners."

For a few minutes they lay quietly together, touching, exploring the sweet sense of discovery between them.

"Sesame seeds, eh?" His voice roughened provocatively as his knee worked its way between hers. "Open, sesame."

She laughed. And then she did.

THE ROOM was cooler and darker when she awakened to the sound of someone moving. The bed beside her was empty but still warm. She sat up to find Jack buttoning his trousers and collecting discarded clothes from the floor and washstand.

"You're leaving?" she said in little more than a whisper.

He paused and looked back at her with a rueful smile.

"It'll be dawn soon, and it wouldn't do for me to be seen sneaking out of your room."

"People might get the right idea," she said tartly, drawing a laugh.

"Exactly."

After a moment he strolled back to her, his naked shoulders swaying in a way that made her breath halt in her throat.

She felt the bed shake as he bumped into it. Or was that just her world quaking with the anticipation of his touch? Bracing on one arm, he bent down to brush her lips with his.

Her eyes closed and that brush bloomed into a wit-draining kiss.

When he pulled away, she swayed and opened her eyes. He was looking at her as if memorizing every detail. Then he touched her hair and let his fingers trail down the side of her face and onto her bare shoulder.

"You know, of course, we can't do this again," he said, his voice husky with both passion and pain.

"We can't?" she said, searching his tumultuous emotions and her own.

"Just once, you said." He straightened, grimly resuming his mantle of responsibility, and headed for the door. As he pulled his greatcoat and hat from the hooks, he turned back. "Our *once* will have to last a lifetime."

The door closed and she felt the ache of loss and longing all the way to her toes. After a moment, her spirits sounded bottom and began to rise.

"Have to last a lifetime?" she echoed. Every nerve in her body rebelled at the thought. "The hell it will. If you think, Jack St. Lawrence, that you've had the last of me, you're wrong."

She bounded from the bed and shivered as she washed and brushed her teeth. By the time she had donned a nightdress, she was remembering everything they'd done and was aching in places she'd forgotten she had.

Wrapping herself in a comforter from the bed, she went to sit by the hearth and stare into the coals glowing in the grate. Taking inventory of her wildly sensitized body, she tried to imagine sharing it with another man, any other man, even one as pleasant as Thomas Bickering. Then came the ultimate test: thinking of her late husband, imagining him here, loving her.

The shudder that overtook her came from deep in her soul. That instinctive, bone-deep reaction told her what she needed to know.

It was Jack St. Lawrence or nobody.

With his deplorable mission he had changed the course of her life. But with those broad shoulders, thirsty kisses and desires he tried so hard and failed so spectacularly to subdue, he had changed *her.*

She was in love with him.

She groaned, feeling that lingering ache between her thighs spreading through her, all the way to her heart. To have him, she would have to risk everything that meant anything to her.

Talk about *consequences.*

JACK FELT a constriction in his chest as he watched her descend the steps into the lobby the next morning. She was wearing one of her Lincoln purchases: a dusky-blue traveling suit cut to enhance each memorable curve and a matching hat with a saucy plume and a veil that added a hint of mystery and put the luscious lips he'd spent half the night exploring beyond his reach. Thank God.

"Good morning," she said with a lilt that set his ears tingling.

He cleared his throat and tried to muster a bit more annoyance.

"What took you so long?" He refused to stare at her veiled features. "We've already missed the 8:11 a.m. and the 9:57 to London. And if we don't hurry, we'll miss the 11:42 and have to wait until 1:30 p.m."

"The eleven-forty-two what?" she asked, drawing on her gloves. He stared, imagining taking them off with his teeth the way she had his.

"Train." He glowered at his reckless thoughts. "We're taking the train to London."

"We are? What about the coach?"

"Too slow," he said shortly, adding in a mutter, "and confining." He turned on his heel and strode off to get one of the bellmen to wrestle her trunk down the stairs and onto a lorry for transport to Cambridge Station.

She not only looked rested, refreshed and renewed—as opposed to his exhausted and exasperated—but seemed utterly immune to his irritable mood. Worse still, she greeted their change of transportation with an acceptance that quickly communicated itself to Mercy, who rattled on about never having been on a train before as they left for the station.

The large yellow-brick station was designed with an impressive arched porte cochere and was large enough to serve three rail lines, despite having only one main track. The lobby bustled with porters, conductors and passengers, every one of whom seemed to look at her as she passed.

If she was aware of the attention she garnered, she didn't show it. She did, however, quietly peruse a few of the well-dressed gentlemen waiting for the London train. Looked them over from stem to stern, in fact.

Jack's hackles rose.

How dare she ogle men as potential acquisitions only hours after making passionate love with him? And how dare *he* have such thoughts after they'd agreed that said love would be "once-in-a-lifetime"?

By the time they were settled in their first-class compartment—watching gentlemen slow to catch glimpses of her—he was roundly irritated. When it occurred to him that one of those men might be the very one to claim her, his hand went possessively to the license in his pocket. He imagined having to hand it—and *her*—over to a slavering merchant or libidinous bureaucrat, and his hands knotted into fists.

She deserved better. She deserved somebody who would

treat her like a lady by day and love her like a courtesan by night. Where was she going to find a man to appreciate her unique sensuality and passion and wit and spirit? Besides him. And where was he going to find a woman who could make him forget touching her, burying his face and hands in her hair…

He sat back and wished he had something—anything—to occupy his mind. He was reminded moments later to be careful what he wished for.

She pulled a pad of paper and a pen from her small valise.

"I thought we should develop a strategy, so as not to waste time and energy in London." She readied her pen. "Where do people of commerce congregate? Bankers, exchange managers, company executives…"

"In the City," he said, trying not to show how the topic rankled. "Government bureaus, banks and stock and commodity exchanges all have their offices in a relatively small borough of London proper."

"Excellent. And I thought perhaps it would be good to see the workings of our fine legal system," she said, making notes. "Where would one go to see barristers and magistrates?"

"The Temple Bar. The Inns of Court are where barristers hang their wigs and silks. The Old Bailey is where trials and lawsuits are heard."

"The Inns of Court, then." More notes. "And our august government…where do those of a political calling spend their time?"

"Besides Parliament and Westminster? Certain gentlemen's clubs are known to serve as the back halls of government." His jaws tightened visibly.

"And physicians? They can always use patronage and support."

"Why don't we just put a 'Husband Wanted' notice in *The Times?*" he snapped irritably.

"You think that would work?" she said with taunting innocence.

He rose, grabbed his hat and excused himself to the smoking car.

Mariah watched him go and sighed, feeling a little ashamed of herself. When she turned to look out the window, she found Mercy glowering at her.

"Ye sure ye got yer heart set on marryin' agin?"

Her heart? That about summed it up.

"I do." She glanced at the door. "Assuming I find the right man."

"Then why don't ye jus' marry Handsome Jack there? He cuts a fine figure. An' he's in the market for a wife."

"Now, *there's* a thought," Mariah said, as if it had never occurred to her.

"Though you'd have to loosen 'im up some." The housemaid scowled as she followed her mistress's gaze to the door. "That lad's cinched up tighter'n a nun's knickers."

"Something tells me he would loosen up nicely—" she gave a knowledgeable smile "—if someone pulled the right strings."

# 14

LATE THAT afternoon, they transferred from the train station by cab to Claridge's in London's fashionable Mayfair district. The hotel had long been known as one of the city's premier lodgings; the ledger bore the names of tycoons, British nobles of every stripe, royalty from the continent and assorted diplomats, heiresses, opera stars and impresarios. *Discretion* was Claridge's watchword, and if there was anything they needed—as Mercy gawked like a bumpkin and Mariah practically had to be frog-marched into that den of luxury—it was discretion.

A word from Jack to the manager secured them two well-appointed rooms at the rear on an upper-level floor.

"Only two?" Mariah questioned him as they signed the register.

"I have my own lodgings in the city."

"You do?" She looked momentarily dismayed, then brightened. "Well, Lord knows I don't need a chaperone." She glanced around the lobby, caught the admiring attention of a fellow dressed like a Prussian general—all Hessians, helmet and gold braid—and returned his interest.

Jack's face tightened as he turned back to the manager.

"We will need *three* rooms, please."

It was intimidating, to say the least, to see the liveried hotel staff scurrying to transport their luggage and packages and arrange for their comfort. But by dinner that night in the hotel restaurant, Mariah had recovered her equilibrium and was able to present to Jack her itinerary for shopping and sightseeing…one that allowed for maximum exposure to London's eligible male population.

Stone-faced and holding the list she had presented him in a death grip, he excused himself before the final course was served and left Mariah to Mercy's rustic company for the rest of the evening.

AT TEN O'CLOCK the next morning, Mariah descended to Claridge's ornate lobby dressed in her military-style navy blue traveling suit and matching toque hat, looking rested and eager to take on the city. Jack had himself just arrived, looking roughly the same color as the gray silk vest he wore beneath an immaculate black suit. The dark circles under his eyes, his somber garments and the dread that had settled over him like a blanket gave him the appearance of a misplaced pall bearer.

Concerned, she suggested they take coffee and offered to find him a headache powder before departing. He donned his top hat, growled that he felt "fine, perfect," and ushered her out to the waiting cab.

The streets were filled with lorries, push carts, omnibuses and foot traffic…all moving at a pace enlivened by the brisk air and unseasonably bright sun. She bent to the window to take in the sights and bombarded him with questions about The Strand, Old Bailey, Big Ben and Parliament.

He watched the way she embraced the city, feeling as if he were seeing her—truly seeing her—for the first time. It was all there: her irresistible vitality, her joy in discovering new things, her irreverent curiosity, her vibrant wit and un-selfconscious beauty.

"Oh, St. Paul's," she said with awe, leaning across his

knees as the cab turned to maintain her view of the cathedral's magnificent dome. "I never thought I'd see it." She looked up with a beaming smile.

He glanced away, feeling as if he'd just stared straight into the sun.

They finally emerged from the cab onto a broad, bustling intersection bounded by official-looking stone buildings and filled with men in business suits and bowlers. The sight brought a gleam to Mariah's eyes.

"So this is the financial heart of the empire, the City," she breathed, grabbing his arm to steady herself after she turned around and around.

"There is the Lord Mayor's residence—Mansion House." He pointed out the looming gray-stone building with the Corinthian-columned portico. "And down there is the Royal Exchange. I thought you might like to see the insurer, Lloyds of London. I have a friend from Cambridge who oversees their underwriting on the electrical-lighting systems cities are starting to install." He halted, seeing a reaction bubbling up in her.

"Just look at all these men." Her eyes lit up. "I mean, you hear the population figures, but it's hard to imagine all these men in one place. Tall ones, short ones…young ones, old ones…rich ones…richer ones…"

He felt—and looked—as if she'd just gored him.

"This way," he ground out, pulling her along toward Lloyds.

So began a day of introductions and cab rides and sights that Mariah had never expected to see: the Royal Exchange, the Tower of London, Waterloo Bridge and Westminster and the Houses of Parliament. Everywhere they went she attracted attention; men interrupted their work in offices and tipped their hats to her in the streets. The more notice she received, the more aloof Jack became. And the more he withdrew, the more pointedly she emphasized their matrimonial mission.

"The gentlemen at the table behind you are staring at me," she said as they sat in a restaurant having a bit of lunch. "Exceedingly fine tailoring. Silk ties and gold pocket watches." She lowered her voice. "Public-school products…I'd lay money on it."

"Shall I go over and demand to know their annual income and inspect their waistcoats for soup stains?" he said with visible annoyance.

"Yes. Please." She directed a small, decorous smile toward the gentlemen in question. "And collect a few ladies' names as references."

He let his fork fall to his plate, drawing her attention back to him.

"Could we have a civil meal just this once," he said in clenched tones, "without you prowling for a mate like a lioness on the Serengeti?"

"My, aren't we judgmental?" she said with unshakeable equanimity. "Especially for a man whose fortunes depend on me finding a 'mate.'"

That set him back on his heels. He had the grace to look chagrined.

"This is not a duty I relish," he said bluntly. "And you make it all the more difficult with your unseemly enthusiasm for the opposite sex."

Mariah studied him for a moment, knowing exactly what was making him chafe and determined to see there would be no relief.

"First I'm too reluctant and overly picky, then I'm too eager and show 'unseemly enthusiasm.' Make up your mind, Jack. Do you want me to find a husband or not?" She watched him struggle internally for control.

"I believe I have made my position on that perfectly clear."

"Yes. But, two days ago," she said, leaving unsaid that it

was before he'd let down his guard and made love to her. Before he'd claimed her in a way no man had before or would after. She studied his frown, wishing she could pry open his head and poke around in his thoughts. She sighed. She'd have to use more conventional methods.

"I have only nine days left to find a husband."

"I am fully aware of the time constraints." He bristled.

"Then how do you suggest I find a good match and make a 'satisfying marriage' if I cannot look at other men or attract their attention?" His silence was gratifying. She let it deepen a bit before delivering the coup de grâce. "Well, I suppose there is always one other option."

"And what would that be?" He went stock-still, listening intently, not allowing himself to meet her gaze.

"You could marry me yourself." *In for a penny, in for a pound.* She produced a demurely wicked grin. "I'm fairly certain we're a match in the 'satisfaction' department."

His jaw loosened and his eyes widened. He looked like a man who'd just had the wind knocked out of him.

"Breathe, Jack. In…out. In…out." She gave his arm a squeeze and laughed.

"It rather puts things into perspective, does it not?" She lifted her chin, knowing the seed had been planted. "Now, about these interesting gentlemen at the next—oh, dear." Her gaze followed the trio of well-dressed men making their way to the door. She let her shoulders sag with disappointment. "They're leaving."

Jack didn't speak another word to her until they were seated in a cab and on the way back to Mayfair for her appointment with a dressmaker. And then it was only to tell her that she would have to dine alone at their hotel that evening since he had business to attend to at his club.

In the long afternoon at the dressmaker's and in the

evening that followed, she had time to go over and over their conversation, trying to tease out the truth of his reaction from the meager clues he'd given. He was shocked and no little alarmed to find himself still wanting her and jealous of the attentions of other men. He didn't want her flirting with, admiring or enjoying other men, but he couldn't bring himself to do anything about it.

The question was: would Iron Jack ever do anything about it?

Thus, she was surprised the next morning to find him entering the hotel breakfast room with a brisk step and a much brighter countenance.

He joined her and Mercy at their table and sipped the strong black coffee the server brought with obvious satisfaction.

"You certainly look better than you did yesterday," she ventured.

"A stroke of luck." His face beamed such seductive pleasure that she was caught unprepared and blindsided by the reason for it. "I made inquiries and discovered Stephens Knitting Mills has a London office...to which Richard Stephens is moving the company." He piled gooseberry jam onto a buttery scone and took a bite, rolling his eyes in appreciation. When he'd washed it down with coffee, he smiled. "Are you ready to meet your future husband?"

"I HAVE an appointment at Le Beau Chapeau at eleven," she said, declining to do more than glance out the cab windows. They were driving through the industrial east end of London, a place filled with factories, warehouses, railway spurs and the din of men and machines loading and unloading freight cars. Was it her imagination, or had dirty, low-hanging clouds deposited themselves over just this part of the city?

"We should be finished here and back in Mayfair in time for you to spend more of the prince's money." He took a fortifying breath and adopted an emphatic glare. "Do try to keep the hat bill to something reasonable."

She refused to rise to the bait.

"Have I mentioned how much I adore the bed linen Claridge's uses? I inquired about it last evening, and the concierge referred me to a department store in Knightsbridge. A place called Harrods. He said they have the finest linen available. If it is good enough for visiting princes, archdukes, and ambassadors, it should be good enough for Bertie. Don't you think?"

She was rewarded by the twitch of a muscle in his jaw.

"It appears Stephens and I have acquaintances in common," he declared, stacking his hands on the head of his walking stick. "It seems he was at Magdalene College in Cambridge some years back. Studied the sciences and engineering. He came not long after I left. His father died in his final year, and he returned home to take charge of the family business."

"A dutiful sort, then." She refused to let his determination daunt her.

"Diligent, I think, might fit better. A fine trait in a husband."

"You think so? What about a wife? Is diligence desirable in a wife?"

"I have never given it any thought." He looked a bit discomfited.

"Well, perhaps it's time you did." She paused a beat. "You know, while we're looking for me a husband, we could look for you a wife."

*"No."*

"Oh, come, Jack, don't be a stuffed shirt. You know, you're far too serious. When you marry, you need to find someone who can make you laugh. You need some humor in your life…along with rampaging passion, tender affection, and a walloping dose of—"

"What I need and don't is none of your concern," he said irritably.

"I was going to say common sense. But I think perhaps you have an oversupply of that already." She studied him openly, tapping her lip thoughtfully with a finger. "I'd say you need someone with a bit of a rebellious streak. Someone who will tempt you to do things you've always wanted to do, but were afraid to try. Someone who will challenge you to live life on your own terms, not on your family's."

*"Enough."*

The force of that word closed the discussion like a sledge hammer. His nostrils flared as he turned to look out the window.

Her heart had just started to find a normal rhythm when the cab stopped and he burst out the door onto the street. She spent a minute gathering her composure, telling herself that he was wrestling with his conflicting impulses. But her spirits were dealt a blow when she ducked out of the carriage to find the driver waiting to assist her instead of Jack.

He'd gone ahead to the door of a plain but imposing brown-brick building with soot-darkened windows set high in the walls. Above the modest street-level door hung a sign identifying Stephens Knitting Mills. Jack tried the handle, then knocked and informed the wool-capped workman who answered that he was there to see Mr. Stephens.

The fellow shrugged and stepped back to allow Jack and Mariah to enter. The place was twice as big inside as it looked from the outside, and it smelled of oil, metal and freshly sawn wood. The cement floor was dotted with machinery pulled from splintered wooden crates that were stacked here and there. Several workmen stood in a surly knot around a fire in a barrel, smoking pipes and casting grim looks at the silent machinery. Directing Jack and Mariah to a set of stairs leading up to a windowed office, the fellow rejoined his comrades.

Jack paused, looking at the stairs.

"Perhaps you should stay here while I see if Stephens is around."

"I need to see him in his element, remember?" she said, eyeing the open steps and pipe-metal railing, then started the climb.

The minute they opened the door, they heard voices and a moan coming from an inner office. Large electric bulbs dangled from the ceiling, illuminating a work area that was just short of chaotic. Half a dozen desks and drafting tables were stacked with boxes and folios and rolled plans, some of which had spilled onto the floor. Wooden filing cabinets with half opened drawers lined two of the walls, and chairs were hidden under piles of paper and the odd greasy machine part.

"Please, sir. Let me send for a physician," came a male voice from the inner room. "You can't go on this way. You have to eat and sleep—"

"I'll take time to eat and sleep when the factory's up and running."

"At this rate, you might not survive long enough to—" The speaker halted, aware of having trespassed.

"I don't care. I'm going to get this factory going if it kills me!"

That raw declaration was so fraught with anguish and pain that Mariah caught Jack's sleeve and looked up at him with alarm. He met her concern with equal uneasiness, then headed for the inner office.

# 15

"EXCUSE ME." Jack stopped in the doorway, taking in the sight of a dismantled machine of some sort spread all over a large desk covered with open blueprints and plans. Mariah peered past his shoulder, gasping at the sight of a tall, excessively slender man braced over the desk and mechanism, looking on the verge of collapse.

The man and his assistant glanced up with surprise.

"We're looking for Richard Stephens, the owner of this enterprise. Perhaps you could tell us if he is on the premises."

"I—I am Richard Stephens." The scarecrow-thin fellow straightened and began to fumble with his vest buttons and to roll down his rumpled sleeves. He glanced miserably around the office, fiddling with his collar and seeming to look for his tie. It was not to be found, but he spotted his coat on a chair beneath some oily machine parts. He closed his eyes briefly and swayed, leaning on the desk. "What can I do for you?"

For a moment Jack just stood there, taking it all in. He was not quick with spontaneous fictions, Iron Jack. But he did make a start.

"Jack St. Lawrence." He tipped his hat and nodded to Mariah. "This is Mrs. Eller. We are...friends of Professor Marcus Jamison of King's College. We were in Cambridge, earlier in the week," he said, slowing, "and...and..."

"The professor was saying what an interesting bit of engineering your new knitting factory was," Mariah provided, slipping past Jack into the room. "He suggested that while we are in London, we should have a look."

Mariah smiled to hide her concern. Stephens's skin was gaunt and pasty, the bags under his eyes were big enough to hold a week's laundry, and his voice rasped ominously. Just standing upright seemed to require a prodigious act of will.

"I fear I'm not in a position to be able to show you anything concrete. There have been…delays." He glanced at the rumpled, bespectacled clerk, who was wringing his hands as if he expected to see his employer crumple at any moment. The worry in his assistant's face seemed to sap the last bit of energy from his pride.

"Damn it all!" He grabbed his stomach. "The power take-offs were damaged in shipping and the gear ratios don't mate with the pattern platens. It's what I get for ordering from more than one machining company. The cursed things don't—aghhh!"

He gasped and doubled over.

Jack and Stephens's assistant both sprang to help and carried him over to a leather sofa buried beneath piles of paper and boxes. Jack swiped the mess onto the floor to make room for Stephens to lie down, and the assistant, Rogers by name, produced a bottle of chalky medicine from a desk drawer and spooned some into Stephens's mouth.

"How long has he been like this?" Jack asked Rogers.

"I'm right here, you know," Stephens said from between gritted teeth.

"Goin' on a week, sir," Rogers answered, wagging his head. "Won't eat nor sleep. He's wearing himself out trying to figure out how to get the lockstitch assemblies aligned and installed."

"It'll just take another day or two," Stephens declared with a burst of defiance. "I'll get it done. Or die trying."

The latter seemed all too real a possibility, Mariah thought, catching Jack's eye, glimpsing his inner conflict and communicating her concern. He turned to stare at the disassembled machine nearby, looking as if he were grappling with, then deciding something.

"This is a variable-speed round-knitter, yes? Electrified?" Removing his hat and dropping his gloves in it, he picked up a set of blueprints and looked them over. "Interesting." He traced lines intently, studying them.

"Have to…make…modifications…" Stephens said, trying to rise. Mariah moved against the edge of the sofa and pushed his shoulders down.

"You'll make nothing but worm food if you don't take care of yourself," she admonished, pulling his haunted brown eyes into hers, praying she could count on what she knew of Jack. "I'm going to send your man for some food, and you're going to eat it and get some rest while Mr. St. Lawrence, here, looks over your plans."

Stephens didn't seem convinced, so she bent close and lowered her voice, such that his eyes opened wider.

"Cambridge man. Something of a prodigy, they tell me." Her tone grew warm and conspiratorial. "He's been feeling itchy and deprived. Let him have a look. It'll do him good."

Then she sealed the deal with a wink.

After Rogers left to fetch some soup and bread from a local tavern, Stephens watched Jack studying his plans and the troubled mechanism and grew anxious. Declaring that he felt much better, he tried to get to his feet.

"Stay where you are." Jack carried the plans to the sofa and knelt beside it to ask for clarifications. Soon they were going over the drawings and specifications together, point by point.

Mariah watched for a while, fascinated by Jack's absorption and willingness to help, then stepped into the outer office to make herself useful. By the time Rogers returned with the food, she had removed her jacket and gloves and begun to straighten the office. She saw to it that Stephens ate his soup and bread and insisted he take some of the thick, dark ale Rogers had procured. As they all hoped, he soon surrendered to the effects of food and drink and sank into an exhausted sleep.

"We should take him home and see him into a proper bed," she said, smoothing Stephens's brow, which was furrowed even in sleep.

"You won't 'see' him anywhere." Jack stood and reached for his hat. "You have an appointment at eleven, remember?"

"But we can't leave him like this." She stared at Jack in disbelief. "He needs help."

"He does indeed. But not the sort you excel in giving." He held open her jacket. "At least not yet. Now get your hat and gloves." When she balked still, he gave a long-suffering sigh. "After I deliver you into the clutches of Fashion, I'm coming back here."

"You are?" She stared at him, her indignation undercut.

"It's a puzzle, actually. And a challenge. But it seems doable. It's been a while since I had a chance to do work of this sort."

Sensing that he meant every word, she slipped into her jacket and reached for her gloves. They said nothing more about Stephens or marriage or the eight days left before her deadline. By the time they reached Le Beau Chapeau she didn't dare look at him, much less speak. Handsome, capable, honorable, compassionate—he was a good man. No, he was the best. And if he caught her gaze, her feelings for him would be plainly visible in it.

Her mind clearly wasn't on hats that afternoon. She scarcely recalled later what she'd purchased or how much money she'd spent. Her thoughts were set on that drafty factory building and the way Jack had volunteered to help Stephens solve his engineering problems. Was that for her benefit or Stephens's? Did it matter which?

When the prearranged cab arrived at four to pick her up, he wasn't in it. Nor was he at tea at the hotel or at dinner later. She was beginning to wonder if his working with Stephens was a good idea. After trying for two hours to write a newsy letter to Carson and her staff at home, she decided to go down to the lobby and purchase a newspaper for diversion.

The lobby was quiet, save for the occasional burst of voices from the bar. While the desk clerk made change for her pound note, she was able to see behind the desk that both keys were still hanging on the hook for Jack's room. He obviously wasn't back yet. Studying the clock over the desk—half-past ten—she decided to wait for him in the lobby and fetched her shawl. Her excuse was valid; she was concerned about Stephens and wanted a report.

Guests came and went, most dressed in evening finery, more than a few well on the way to intoxication. It was a full hour later when Jack came through the doors of the hotel with his suit coat hanging over one shoulder, carrying his vest and tie. He paused by the night doorman to remove his hat and peel away his coat. His shirtsleeves were rolled up and his hair was a mess. She rose, taking him in, thinking that she'd never seen a more beautiful man.

He spotted her standing by one of the columns, wrapped in a large, soft shawl, and he halted. His face filled with both fatigue and pleasure.

"How did it go?" she asked, approaching him.

"Well, actually. We arranged to have some of the fittings reground and drafted a new layout for the factory floor. Stephens is quite good with machines and processes. He was just too exhausted to think straight."

"So it's going to be all right?" She held her breath. His smile burst over her like the first bold rays of a warm spring sun.

"I think he's going to have a highly profitable operation there."

"And his health?"

"He dozed between jobs this afternoon. As I was leaving, I sent him home with Rogers for some much-needed sleep. He'll be right as rain in a couple of days. I'm going back Friday to help him install the equipment."

"Jack, you're—that's wonderful!" Unable to resist the joy flooding through her, she threw both arms around him. Shocked at first, he picked her up and whirled her around, his quiet, deep-chest rumble so rich and welcome that she couldn't bring herself to remind him where they were. He finally realized it himself and set her on her feet. Since the lobby was deserted, he kept his arms around her for a moment to savor the feeling.

"Look at you." She stroked the smile-creased plane of his cheek.

"Just don't inhale. I probably reek." He winced. "My shirt is full of sweat and oil and sawdust, and these trousers— You don't want to hear what I crawled through on the factory floor and climbed through in the rafters to work on the electrical wiring."

"Don't disillusion me." She wrinkled her nose. "I think you smell wonderful, even with the— Did you say you worked on electrical wires?"

"I did."

"Jack! Electricity is dangerous. You could have been killed."

"Not really. I've studied it, experimented in the lab at Cambridge. I just never had a chance to get my hands on a real application until now."

She lifted his hands, shocked by the scratches and grease on them.

"What would your family say if they could see you?" she said, aware of the broader context, realizing how important the afternoon had been.

"Fortunately—" he grinned "—none of them are within fifty miles. You know, there will soon be a huge market for electrical motors. I talked to Stephens about it and he agreed it would be a prime investment. If I get my hands on some capital…"

He turned her toward the stairs, keeping an arm around her waist as they climbed up them. They fell silent as they neared their rooms and paused in the darkened hallway, both feeling the elemental pull of desire.

"About Stephens." She took a small but significant step back. It had to be said. "I'm not going to marry him."

He looked down, shuttering his eyes.

"I guessed as much. Not really your type."

She saw that familiar twitch in his jaw and braced, expecting a reminder, lecture or out-and-out rebuke. But he didn't continue or look up.

"Well…" She gave an unsteady laugh. "You know how I like—"

"Muscles. Right."

"And lots of—"

"Hair. Thick, soft hair."

His controlled voice gave no hint of how this exasperated him, but at least his hands weren't clenched into fists.

"So, you don't have to help Stephens on my account."

"What makes you think I'm doing it for you?" He glanced up, giving her a flash of the emotion roiling inside him, then looked down again. "It's a challenge." Passion crept into every word. "Something I *like* to do, something I'm damned good at. The professor was right. I haven't done what I want to do, what I *need* to do in too damned long." He took a shuddering breath. "You said it, too. And you were right."

Her heart began to pound as she absorbed what he was saying, and she felt hope uncoiling in her middle and threading through her. Whole universes of possibility were born in the silence that followed.

"There's something else you need to do, Jack." Her mouth dried as she read the moment and knew the time had come.

"What is that?" he said in that same carefully neutral tone.

She swallowed hard.

"Make me yours."

The words hung in the dark, intimate atmosphere of the hall. For the first time in her adult life, she wanted to run. The suspense was unbearable.

Then he looked up and she said it again…into those molten eyes.

"Make me yours, Jack."

His gaze sank into hers.

And set her on fire.

His mouth descended on hers, his arms lashed her to him like steel bands and his body—hot and hard against hers— demanded a response.

Heat exploded in her, flinging sparks along her nerves. Every part of her was suddenly alive and hungry. She met his kiss and pulled him into her, deepening the contact, yielding and demanding at the same time.

Somehow they made it to her door and he managed to take her key from her, put it into the lock and turn it—proof of mad mechanical skills if there ever was one. He backed her into the room and closed the door with his foot, since his hands were busy touching her everywhere he could reach.

Her shawl hit the floor and he started on her blouse buttons. She dispensed with his braces, pulled his shirt out, and managed to unbutton his trousers while helping him dispatch her skirt. She had a few skills herself.

Suddenly they were skin to skin, bare arms and shoulders, kissing and swaying wildly, trembling with eagerness. She could barely breathe by the time she stepped out of her petticoats and kicked them away. When she stepped out of her shoes, he lifted his head.

"Leave the shoes," he muttered against her throat. "I like shoes."

"And stockings?" she said on a breathy laugh.

"And stockings."

"What about corsets?"

He pulled back and looked at her breasts with lust so potent that her sex turned liquid. He inserted a finger beneath that rim of pink satin, and with a deft motion, flicked her nipple free. He took that one into his mouth as he freed the other. She squirmed with response and he laughed.

"The corset stays." He ran his hands over her bound waist and peeled her knickers down, while staring at the nipples peeking over her boning. "You look like a *petit four.* All smooth white frosting and pink rosettes." He did what was natural with those velvety rosettes—devoured them.

When her knees buckled, he caught her and bore her back to the bed, never ceasing his attention on her breasts. She welcomed him between her thighs and felt his erection slide into the wet, burning cleft of her flesh. Every motion answered a need she hadn't realized she possessed. Soon the combination of his mouth on her breasts and the tantalizing *almost* of his sex at the opening of hers had brought her to the brink of climax.

"Jack," she gasped, clasping him with her legs. "*Now,* Jack."

Tilting, she urged him inside and moaned with pleasure as he filled and stretched her, pushing deeper, thrusting all the way to her core. As she gripped his shoulders and pulled him still tighter against her, he began to move and give her the pressure and sensation she craved. Soon he was drumming toward climax, calling her name. When he would have withdrawn, she wrapped her legs tighter and forbade it, holding him inside her. Then every barrier of time and place and sensation burst between them.

She heard a groan through the fury of her own pleasure, and couldn't tell if it was hers or his. Everything seemed to be happening inside her skin; his release somehow complemented and enhanced hers.

He collapsed over her and she felt a hiss of steam run through her blood. The fire was well and truly quenched. For now.

"Elbows," she said, smiling at the way he still bore part of his weight on his arms. "You are such a gentleman."

"The least I could do," he said with a rueful laugh, "considering my appalling eagerness." He would have shifted to lie beside her, but she held him for a moment longer, giving him an intimate squeeze with her inner muscles that made him jump with surprise.

"You never have to apologize to me for how you like your pleasure, Jack. Fast, slow, on a chair, against a wall, in a carriage…in nightcaps and flannel shirts or masks and transparent silk…say what you desire. I'll make it happen if I can. I'm yours."

He brushed a wisp of her hair back and searched her face with wonder.

"You're unbelievable, Mariah. What am I going to do with you?"

"I have a few suggestions," she said with a demure smile.

"Which I'll be pleased to take…when I come back."

The bed heaved and he was off before his withdrawal registered.

"You're going?" She sat up feeling rattled and a little disoriented. "Now? Why?"

He picked up his trousers and came back to the bed as

he dragged them on. Bending down, he kissed her gently on the lips.

"I'm going to bathe. I'll be back in fifteen minutes. And then I expect to continue this most enlightening conversation."

As the door closed behind him, she lay back on the bed, stretched, and smiled. She'd declared herself, more or less. She was his.

But was he hers?

# 16

MAKE ME YOURS, she'd said. He had. And he was going to again, and there wasn't a second thought or an ounce of regret in his body.

He stared at his lathered face in the mirror, holding his razor poised. He was grinning like a lovesick fool. She made him feel whole and real; grounded him and set him soaring at the same time. She reminded him of the things he wanted and loved and was good at doing. She had become the voice of his hopes and dreams and desires, not to mention his conscience.

What was he going to do with her?

Whatever he decided, it would be better than doing without her. For once, he was not going to be sensible and abstemious and self-denying. For once he was going to do what his heart told him. He was going to make love to her and enjoy her and figure out the rest when he had to. Later. Much, much later.

Hurrying through a bath and a shave, he put on fresh trousers and shirt and a pair of slippers, then wrapped himself in a dressing gown. When he slipped back into her room, he found she had lit a lamp and donned a thin silk dressing gown. She had let down her hair, then looped it up into a soft mass of curls. At his entry, she turned and paused in front of the lamp, unwittingly creating an erotic silhouette of her half-naked body. She had left the corset and stockings on. He smiled.

"I thought you should see what I got today," she said,

taking him by the hand and pulling him to the stuffed chair by the hearth. "Sit."

A moment later she pulled a sophisticated little velvet toque from a hatbox against the wall. She donned it and strode back and forth, describing it with clench-jawed hauteur. He enjoyed the mimicry, but appreciated even more the way she forgot to hold her dressing gown together and casually displayed the erotic territory she'd invited him to claim.

Next came a picturebook hat…wide-brimmed, romantic and awash in ribbons and flowers. Her demeanor changed to wide-eyed innocence.

"Please, sir, could you direct me to a reputable boarding-house? I'm a country girl just come to town, and I don't know anyone in this big, frightening city." She fluttered her lashes and made an outrageous moue. He laughed wickedly and grabbed her, pulling her between his knees.

"Just put yourself in my hands, sweetness." He slipped his hands around her bum cheeks and then ran his fingers through the sensitive muff at the top of her legs. "Uncle Jack will teach you how to get along."

She giggled softly and shivered. Then she bent to lick his lips with a provocative purr.

"Naughty Uncle Jack."

She pulled away abruptly, and as he protested, strode to another hat box and pulled out a handsome felt derby and a riding crop. She strutted back and forth, smacking the crop against her palm, staring at him as if she could peel his scruples like a grapefruit.

"Of course, you realize I brook no disobedience from my mounts," she said with a velvety roughness to her voice. "I ride hard and long and I expect my horses to be in prime condition to give me pleasure. You think you can remember that, stable boy?"

His jaw dropped. His erection crowned. He couldn't speak, couldn't take his eyes from the mesmerizing sway of her hips as she stalked closer and used the tip of her crop to lift his chin. When she lowered her mouth to his, he nearly exploded there and then.

It was a hard, possessive kiss that inflamed every nerve in his body.

"Well?" She stared down into his simmering golden eyes.

"Your mount is ready to ride, mistress," he said, running a hand up her leg and cupping her buttock. "Anytime you want."

With a smile that was part triumph, part mischief, she slanted a leg across him and slid down astride his lap. Rubbing purposefully against his erection, she groaned with pleasure. Or maybe he did. It was hard to tell.

A moment later she was kissing him with all the hunger she'd just generated in him. And when she came up for air, she was grinning.

"What do you think of my purchases?"

"I think—" he was hoarse with need "—I'm not ever letting you go shopping alone again."

He gasped as she peeled his trousers aside and slid her hand up and down the length of him. A moment later she slid her slick, swollen flesh up and down him, too. With a growl of appreciation, he pulled her head down to kiss her long and hard. It wasn't long before they transferred to the bed and the riding continued in earnest. With her on top.

Later, as they lay together in a sea of feathers and felt and silk and flowers, she pushed up onto an elbow to trace his features with her fingers.

"I don't think you should get your expectations too high about shopping. Very few milliners are open-minded enough to let this sort of thing go on in their shops."

He laughed. "I would guess so." He looked at the hats she'd tried on and thought of the personas that came with them. "Which is your favorite?"

She rolled up onto her knees and sat back on her heels. One by one, she picked up the hats, smoothing a flower here and stroking a feather there.

"I like them all," she said thoughtfully, dragging a feather down his belly. He jolted, grabbed her hand to stop the tickling, then sought her gaze.

"Which one is the true you?" he asked softly.

She thought about that for a moment, her blue eyes darkening.

"None of them, I think. The true me is what you see before you now. No frills. Just me. Bare head. Naked body." He saw the moment she dropped the last guard to her heart. It took his breath.

"I love you, Jack St. Lawrence. That's the real me."

He was on his knees in a heartbeat, holding her face between his hands, absorbing her words into his very marrow, struggling with and then surrendering to the stubborn, possessive joy in his heart. He couldn't let clever, adorable, surprising, stubborn, passionate and loving Mariah Eller walk down the aisle and out of his life. He was going to have to be at the end of that church aisle himself. He was going to have to marry her. His heart would refuse to beat ever again if he didn't.

"That's a gift more precious than I deserve, Mariah Eller," he said, refusing to think about the ramifications yet. "But I'll cherish it for as long as I draw breath. And I pray that someday I'll be worthy of it."

CLARIDGE's lobby had indeed been deserted when Jack walked through the front doors, but the bar was not. A second pair of eyes had caught sight of him the moment he entered.

Baron Marchant was making an early evening of losing at his favorite gaming salon. Bertie had asked him to escort some inebriated Prussians back to their hotel and they had insisted he join them for a drink. He thought it only fitting that he accept; it was his damned money they were spending.

One of the Prussians, sunk deep in his cups, began reciting a maudlin-sounding epic about some heroic battle…in German. Marchant was doing his best to enjoy the brandy in spite of the wretch's blathering, when he spotted a familiar figure entering the hotel.

St. Lawrence. His spirits lifted. The fellow was something of a stick in usual company, but he would be a vast improvement over this gloomy lot. He rose to intercept Jack, but stopped inside the bar entrance when he heard a woman's voice say Jack's name. Moving instinctively to the side of the opening, he blinked and put in his monocle to make her out.

Memory and deduction came together to boot Marchant's brain.

The widow? St. Lawrence had brought her here? To London? His jaw dropped as the Prince of Wales's latest conquest threw her arms around Jack, and Jack embraced her and whirled her around like a giddy schoolboy. In the middle of Claridge's lobby!

Marchant's eyes burned with the need to blink, but he continued to stare at her. Mariah Eller was beaming at Jack with a directness that spoke of intimacy. When she reached up to stroke his face, they turned just enough for Marchant to make out his expression.

Gone were the fierce aura of control, the subtle arrogance, the moral superiority that had never failed to annoy the prince's other intimates. Iron Jack, they called him behind his back. The standards-keeper. Right now his aristocratic features were filled with the same idiotic pleasure as hers.

*Sweet Jesus.*

Jack was bedding the prince's light o' love! The one he and Jack had been charged with marrying off. From the looks of them, there was more than just a bit of slap-and-tickle going on. It was a full-blown *romance.*

He watched them walk toward the stairs, Jack holding her adoringly, the widow gazing up at him as if he were the blessed Second Coming.

Iron Jack was in love.

Marchant leaned against the door frame and scoured his face with his hands, trying to sober up enough to figure out what to do. There would be hell to pay when Bertie found out about this. Bertie liked St. Lawrence—liked the whole damned St. Lawrence family. He'd want to blame someone else. Someone charged with securing the widow's cooperation. He felt his collar tighten.

Somebody had to talk to Jack, make him see the error of his ways—and soon, before hints of this reached Bertie's ears.

Inspiration struck. *Family.* That was what St. Lawrences prized above all else. Jack's eldest brother Jared lived just west of London.

If he left first thing in the morning he could be there by noon.

ONCE THEY were married, he was going to have to foot these bills, Jack thought the next morning as he stood in a shoe shop, watching her wade through a sea of shoes: house slippers, day boots, pumps, slides, walking shoes, riding boots…French heels, wedges…kid, satin, brocade and patent leather. It was sobering, even worrisome in light of the fact that his family would likely disown him. But the sight of her shapely ankles burned itself into his brain and he soon was aching to carry her back to their hotel and ravish her within an inch of her life.

Colliding with Mercy's glare doused that untimely ardor. The salty old servant was looking at him as if he had grown a second head.

Was it his imagination that the head porter at the hotel had stared at him oddly, too? And that the waiter in the breakfast room seemed to find him suddenly amusing? He checked his trouser buttons, collar and glanced at his hair in a lobby mirror. Finding nothing amiss, he'd shrugged it off.

Then there was that officious wretch at the linen draper's shop, who kept ogling Mariah as if she were made of sugar. That he could understand. She was pure honey-blond radiance. Sunlight trapped in human form. He found himself smiling wistfully at her and feeling a little foolish...but only until she smiled back and he felt his heart swell.

Things improved after a bracing cup of tea and some sweets and savories in a Knightsbridge tea room. But they were soon off to the dressmaker's to check on the progress of her purchases, and he was back to holding packages and nodding politely. She insisted he see every style she chose, which meant he had to sit idly in the close, over-perfumed fitting room with Mercy...who kept looking askance at him.

Something was bubbling to the old servant's surface. He tried to ignore it, but she dropped the carpet bag she habitually carried and a thimble rolled out and across the polished floor. He was forced by both breeding and conscience to retrieve it...which brought him face to face with her.

"Don't think it ain't writ all over ye," she whispered with a scowl.

"What is 'writ' all over me?" he said, under the misapprehension that she wouldn't dare raise a truly personal topic with him.

"How ye spent last evenin'," she whispered, eyes darting at the fitting-room doorway. "I ain't blind, ye know. I just got the lumbago."

After a week closed up in a coach, train and sundry cabs with her betters, familiarity apparently *had* bred contempt.

"How I spent the evening?" He stiffened, gripping the knob of his walking stick. "I worked at the Stephens factory until nearly midnight."

"I heard ye, late, in th' hall."

"I have no idea what you're on about."

"Shame on ye, sarr. She be a decent woman havin' to get married 'cause o' money troubles." She squared her shoulders, looking as if she'd just eaten a sour persimmon. "Ye want her carryin' a bundle to th' altar?"

"Don't be ridiculous." He could feel himself paling. *A bundle?*

"Plain as th' hair on the old Queen's chin, it is. Yer glowin' like daisies, the both of ye."

"Really, this is *most* improper," he said, trying for the glower that had never failed to put servants in their place, until now.

"Marry the lass, sarr. Make a honest woman o' her." Her tone was sharp enough to draw blood. "Or make yer John Thomas happy yerself."

Jack froze, hearing the first words echoing in his head and telling himself surely he had mistaken the last. Make an honest woman of her.

*Marry the lass, sarr.*

Hearing those words spoken outside his head was jarring.

The harsh light of logic fell on the sweet, irrational hope of his heart.

Marrying Mariah. The whole of his life was weighted against it. His family expected him to turn Bertie's favor and influence into a marriageable asset. But he'd failed to carry out Bertie's special mission and—worse—usurped Bertie's pleasure. He'd seen how the prince cut off men and families who failed to show him proper respect. He didn't want to imagine the prince's outrage upon learning that Jack had wedded the woman he had claimed as his mistress.

The day's bright prospect suddenly dimmed.

There was no way to have both her and the prince's favor.

# 17

Mariah stepped out from behind the changing screen in a half-sewn blue satin dinner gown that displayed her figure to spectacular advantage. She twirled around, holding the train up as she might while waltzing.

"What do you think?" she asked, coming to a stop in front of them.

"A pure vizhun, miz." Mercy beamed.

"Needs more fabric." Jack stared at her bared bosom. "A *lot* more."

She gave a throaty laugh and her eyes danced with a hint of mischief.

"Well, I am reliably informed that this style is *de rigueur* for ladies of quality at fine restaurants and the opera."

"Ever *been* to an opera?" he asked with exaggerated distaste. "The audience should be allowed to wear nightcaps and bedclothes."

She burst into laughter and gripped the waist of the gown as if afraid the temporary stitching might not hold. He joined her, and after a moment, so did Mercy, though she seemed to be wondering what she was laughing about. When they sobered, Mariah settled a warm smile on him.

She didn't know when she'd felt so good or enjoyed someone's company as much as she did Jack's. He constantly surprised her with droll comments on London society. In him, a lively curiosity was mated with a rebellious and rigorous intellect that viewed matters from odd angles. The result was that he, like the rest of the male sex, was beset by internal contradictions that sometimes embarrassed him.

He was supremely self-controlled, but he was as fond of pleasure as any man alive. He refused to subscribe to popular thought without critical analysis, but he was careful to observe social conventions as though they were immutable laws. It was as if outward conformity was the price he paid to allow himself the freedom to think and feel for himself.

Wanting her was the ultimate expression of that tension inside him. To admit he loved her would be to risk losing the benefits of birth and social standing he'd enjoyed his entire life. To have her, to truly make her his, he would have to turn his comfortable, predictable world on its ear.

*Do you love me that much, Jack?* she asked with her eyes. *You've pulled me from my safe, secure life and made me want a love, a family, a lifetime with you. Are you willing to leave your safe, secure world to have those things with me?*

His ragged, desire-filled sigh muted every worry clamoring inside her. Being with him, wanting him and loving him…that was what was important. They had a week left. Seven days. It might be selfish, but she wanted every precious minute of every precious one of them with him.

Promising Jack an easier time of it at Harrods, Mariah shopped next for the fine linens and pillows she had developed such a fondness for at the hotel. The store was elegant and overwhelming…packed ceiling to floor with fine foods, elegant china, figurines, clothing, inventions and household items of every purpose and description.

Mercy complained of her lumbago and seemed on the

verge of her first ever collapse due to "vapors," when Mariah discovered some adorable bonnets. The parlor maid cum traveling companion was miraculously revived by a new hat and a finely crafted pair of walking shoes.

The rest of the day they spent seeing more of London's sights by carriage: Hyde Park, the Crystal Palace and, for good measure, Madame Tussaud's Wax Museum. There, they disembarked and paid for admission. Mercy required smelling salts outside the Chamber of Horrors and refused to continue the tour. They left her in a lady-seat by the entry and went on to see the rest of the exhibits…holding hands when they were out of her sight, and talking and laughing with their heads together, looking very much like the lovers they were.

Later, during tea at the hotel, Jack conferred with the concierge and returned to the table to announce he had acquired tickets to a concert at Royal Albert Hall. Mariah couldn't speak as she stared at the tickets he presented her. When she looked up, she knew her pleasure shone in her eyes.

"I recall how much you like music," he said wryly.

"I do indeed." She grinned. "An orchestra at Royal Albert Hall!" She had a sobering thought. "But I don't have an evening dress to wear."

"Sunday clothes will do. It's a large hall and not half so socially demanding as the opera."

"Ye'll be needin' me to come." Mercy speared Jack with a look. "Right?"

He exhaled quietly.

"Of course." Mariah spread the tickets in a fan to show that Jack had indeed purchased three.

That was how they came to be sitting that night in the vast, gaslit expanse of the empire's crowning architectural wonder. It was an oval-shaped amphitheater capable of seating thousands in classical opulence, but tonight, the hall was far from full. Jack had been able to get prime seats on the tier just above the main floor and fairly near the stage.

They arrived in time for a quick tour, but not in time for a ride in one of the hydraulic lifts that carried patrons up to the art-filled gallery that ringed the uppermost level. That, Jack declared, would have to wait until intermission. When Mercy learned that a hydraulic lift was essentially a box in which you rode a hundred feet straight up, she looked a bit conflicted and then declared she was willing to forego that excitement.

As the musicians took the stage and the lights dimmed, Mariah put her hand on Jack's arm and left it there throughout the first two selections. As the varied program continued with works from Brahms, Beethoven and Liszt, she spent as much time watching Jack as she did the performers.

The dim lighting and evocative music of so many strings gave the experience an intimacy that made Mariah long to be someplace not so public. When she looked up at Jack, the sight of his jawline sent a ripple of sexual excitement through her that made her gasp. He turned to see what had caused it and she lowered her eyes, a bit embarrassed.

She clasped her hands and pressed her knees together, taking deep, slow breaths. Fortunately the music slowed and grew dreamy and pastoral. She was starting to relax, when a snort from Mercy made her jump. She turned and Jack leaned out to look past her at the maid…who was snoring.

"Brahms," Jack whispered with a chuckle. "He does it every time."

When the lights came up at intermission, Mercy roused, blinked, and allowed herself to be persuaded to sit while they stretched their legs with a trip to the Gallery. As they waited in line for the lift, Mariah was even more aware of Jack's handsome male presence and grew a little breathless.

They stepped out and began to walk along the broad, art-lined Gallery. Longing shot through her as she saw and felt his muscular strides and the subtle sway of his shoulders. Her body vibrated with a delicious private knowledge of the sexual prowess of the man at her side.

When they stopped with a small group of other theater-goers to study a painting, she settled herself in front of him and brushed the front of his trousers. A flash of desire rushed through her, brightening her eyes. She felt him stiffen, though his expression didn't change. Then he leaned to her ear, his eyes lidded and unreadable.

"You are a naughty girl, Butterfly," he whispered.

She smiled and struck off for another painting. Under the guise of making room for other patrons, he pressed against her back…and ran a hand up the side of her waist. Yet another painting and their legs brushed. Still another, and she turned and slid by him, body pressed to body, hand dragging covertly over the ridge developing in his trousers.

"A pity they don't have a tea room here," she said, glancing out over the hall itself. "I would love some tea and a *petit four*. How about you?" She flicked a gaze at him from the corner of her eye. "Would you like a luscious little cake with white frosting and taut pink rosettes?"

He pulled her behind a large potted palm and kissed her. She laughed and ducked out of his embrace to stroll further down the gallery. He was only a step behind her as she paused before another painting.

"Perhaps I can arrange a little tea party in my room tonight," she said quietly, feigning absorption in the rather garish landscape.

"Wicked woman," he muttered next to her ear. "I'm already—"

"*St. Lawrence?*" A strident male voice shattered that delicious moment. They started apart and looked around to locate the source.

"It *is* you!" A familiar face had appeared a few yards away in the middle of the gallery. "I thought you were somewhere in the country, growing moss."

The dapper, elegant man Mariah had hosted in her inn as Jack A. Dandy was suddenly closing on them with a bluff, confident smile and an outstretched hand. She stifled the urge to hide her still-tingling lips and straighten her clothes.

"Cranmer. Imagine seeing you here." Jack's chin rose as he retreated into well-practiced reserve. "I never took you for a music lover."

"Well, you know how it is." The dapper earl gave a wicked grin and tossed a glance over his shoulder to indicate several men gathered around a portly figure in a dark suit. "Where *he* goes, we go."

Mariah's heart stopped as her gaze fell on the group's central figure. He was of average height, considerable girth and sported a closely cropped pointed beard that she recalled all too well.

*"St. Lawrence?"* the prince called.

The heir to the throne and his companions bore down on them from across the gallery. Her first impulse was to run, to grab Jack's hand and just flee for her life. But Jack was planted firmly at her side with his hand searching between them for hers. A brief squeeze was all he could manage before the prince and his men were upon them.

"And Mrs. Eller. What an unexpected pleasure!" Bertie's face lit as he reached for her with both hands. She laid her hands in his and gave a small curtsy. "What a sight you are— even lovelier than I remembered. What the devil are you doing here in London?" This last he aimed equally at Jack, who stood at attention.

Jack didn't look at her; he was focused fully on the prince.

"Seeing the sights, Your Highness, and shopping," she answered for them both. Her face felt as though it might crack from the force a smile required.

"And taking care of a certain legal matter," Jack added.

"By God, you look scrumptious. Doesn't she, lads?" There was enthusiastic agreement as he looked her over thoroughly and introduced her to his group, which included Jack Ketch and Jack Sprat and Jack A. Dandy. Titled men, every one. "Quite a stunner you're escorting here, Jack."

"So she is, Your Highness," Jack responded. With a countenance now resembling granite, he made no move to interfere as the prince transferred her hand to his arm so he would be free to clasp her waist. But then she spotted a familiar twitch in Jack's jaw…saw his hand curl into a fist.

Gordon Clapford's bloodied face rose in her mind, and her heart lurched back to duty, racing to make up for lost time.

"Well, my dear, have you found our fair city to your liking?"

Sliding determinedly into the worldly persona that had allowed her to handle the prince before, she managed to wedge her arm between herself and Bertie's middle and make a bit of room.

"I cannot speak for the entire city, Highness, since I haven't seen it *all.* But I certainly have found Harrods a delight." She hoped her eyes twinkled. It must have worked; the prince and his companions seemed charmed. "Do you know they have telephones? I had never seen one. And an American phonograph that plays recorded music and political speeches."

"Political speeches?" The prince laughed heartily. "Pray that doesn't catch on. There's entirely too much 'speechifying' in politics as it is."

"And this afternoon, we took in Madame Tussaud's Wax Museum. Quite the chilling experience, if I do say so. My maid, Mercy, was quite overcome and had to be revived with smelling salts."

There was more laughter, which would have been a relief if the prince hadn't chosen that moment to turn to Jack.

"Where are you keeping her, St. Lawrence?"

"Claridge's," Jack said tautly.

"Excellent. Know it well." A canny look came over the prince. "You needn't worry. I'll see she gets home safe and sound." He tucked Mariah's hand into the crook of his arm. "Come, my dear. Let's have a stroll and see a bit more of this *art*."

# 18

IT COULDN'T have been clearer that Jack was being dismissed. Mariah tried to catch his eye, but his gaze was lowered as he nodded, backed a step, and then turned on his heel. She watched him head for the lift with a sick feeling. It was all she could do to attend to the prince's question.

"So, is Jack looking after you well?"

"Yes," she said, afraid to say more lest her voice give away her feeling for him. As they walked, the prince's companions began to fall discreetly away. Soon, with only Jack Sprat and Jack A. Dandy for company, Bertie began to explore his latest acquisition.

"And what of the legal matter Jack mentioned?" the prince asked as his hands drifted over her. "Has that been settled to your satisfaction?"

"Interesting that you should mention that, Highness."

"Bertie, please," he said, leaning so close that she could smell the tobacco and brandy on his breath.

"*Bertie.* It seems we've run into a bit of a snag. There were four possibilities on the list—but I mustn't bore you with such details."

"No, no, I want to know. I am deeply interested in your welfare, my dear." His hand tightened on her waist and his voice lowered. *"Deeply."*

"The first candidate, a solicitor from Lincoln, was already

contracted to marry someone else…well and truly off the market. The second prospect, the soon-to-be Baron Clapford, was an arrogant, overwhelming boor, who very nearly cold-cocked me when we met."

"He what?" Bertie stopped dead, drawing the others to a halt.

"Clapford? The MP from Grantham? He's got a nasty temper," Jack Sprat declared, "but I wouldn't have taken him for a woman bully."

"To be fair, I pushed him into his fish pond first." They gaped at her. "In my defense, I thought he was going to hit me. So, it was instinctive, not malicious." The prince hooted and she realized that laughter was the key to forestalling his advances. "I don't think you should count on getting any fancy goldfish from him to stock your garden ponds, Your Highness."

"I'll remember. No goldfish," he said, grinning. "Surely there was someone more suitable."

"We went to Cambridge next, where I met Professor Winston Martindale of Magdalene College."

"Martindale? Wait—I know that name." Bertie looked to Sprat and Dandy for help. "Where do I know that name from?"

They shook their heads.

"Your husband list?" she prompted. "It seems he's been on it before. Winston Martindale, of the deplorable dental hygiene?"

"Oh, my God!" Bertie recalled with shock. "Toothless Winnie! He's still around?" He looked to the others, who apparently also recalled the professor. "Who the devil gave Jack old Winnie Martindale's name?"

The others were too busy laughing to reply.

"I believe it was the Earl of Chester's son," she ventured.

"I might have known." Bertie looked genuinely annoyed.

"But Martindale is no longer toothless," she said brightly.

"He has a new set of teeth from Germany. 'If you ever need a new set of choppers,' he said, 'the Huns make the very best.'" She made her bucktoothed face. "You should see them. Big as fence posts." The prince's friends leaned against the wall, weak with laughter. "He's generous with them, too. Took them out and offered to let me give them a try."

She was laughing such that she had to wipe the corners of her eyes.

"I declined. Seeing as half his dinner was still in them."

"Ha-ha-ha-ha-haaarghh!" Bertie laughed so hard he started to cough. The others patted him on the back, until he got control and waved them off.

When he'd sobered, he settled a perceptive gaze on her.

"You're quite an unexpected treat, my dear. Don't know when I've laughed like that." He pulled out his handkerchief, dabbed his eyes, then took her arm through his again. "So, who did you finally settle on?"

She winced.

"No one, I'm afraid."

He halted to look at her, holding her arm a bit too tightly.

"You mean to say you have no plans to marry?" The consequences of that were made plain as his fleshy features sharpened and his eyes took on a cool displeasure. She couldn't allow him to think Jack had failed.

"Well, as it happens, I do have a matrimonial candidate in mind. Someone quite acceptable to me. But—" she gave him her most appealing smile "—I fear you may not approve. And I do so want you to approve."

"Don't be silly." His affability returned in a rush that made it less than convincing. "I'm sure anyone you want will be perfectly fine with me. After all, my dear, I want you to be happy. He will make you happy, won't he?"

"I believe so. I mean, he's not a handsome prince." She

sighed, hoping he would be flattered. "But, I think there's enough there to work with. Given time, I can shape him into a suitable husband."

"Consider it done, then. If you think he'll do, then by all means marry the blighter." He leaned closer, and closer still. *"The sooner the better."*

It was only then that she realized he had maneuvered her into a niche between a column and a large potted palm. The music had resumed in the concert hall, drawing the rest of the audience back to the hall. They were virtually alone.

His mouth descended on hers and the wrongness of it shocked her motionless.

If she had ever entertained any notion of complying with the prince's demands and becoming his mistress, that kiss would have quashed it. His lips were thick and rubbery and his mouth was beard-scratchy and wet; she was simultaneously drowning and being devoured! Only the strongest self-control allowed her to remain trapped in his embrace.

When he raised his head, his features were coarsened by lust alloyed with power.

"And what is the name of this lucky lump you've decided to mold into a domesticated male?"

She prayed she wasn't making the mistake of her life.

"Jack St. Lawrence."

Her heart stopped as he froze. The surprise on his face deepened, and he pulled away and looked her up and down.

*"My* Jack St. Lawrence?" he said, clearly taken aback. After what seemed a small eternity, he produced a smile that didn't reach his eyes.

"Have you spoken with him about this?" he demanded.

"Heavens, no. I haven't mentioned the word *marriage*. He's not the most conversational of fellows. Besides, I believe it's always best to let a man think matrimony is *his* idea."

She gave a nervous laugh that she didn't have to fake.

"If you have someone better, I'd be happy to entertain another option. I have another whole week, I believe." She ran a flirtatious finger down the buttons of his waistcoat. "To prepare."

"It's just…Jack St. Lawrence. It's somewhat unexpected. He's not known to be much of a ladies' man."

"Precisely what will make him a proper and dutiful husband. A man who is too successful with the ladies finds it difficult to be satisfied with the monotony of home life." She slipped her arm through his and pressed against his shoulder to distract him from realizing that *he* was the prime example of that axiom. As they turned toward the lift she assured him, "Trust me, Highness. I have experience in these matters."

JACK HAD STUMBLED from the lift and managed to make his way back to the seats he and Mariah had shared minutes earlier. Images of her trapped at Bertie's side blinded him to all but the most rudimentary of sensory input. He collected the protesting Mercy, bundled her into a cab and deposited her on Claridge's doorstep…then headed for his club and a bottle of Scotch.

Halfway through the first glass he found it impossible to swallow any more of the stuff. He'd failed her, failed himself, even failed Bertie in a way. If he'd been truthful about that night at the inn, Bertie wouldn't have started this whole damnable thing. And if he'd kept his hands and his lips to himself…

…*he'd be even more miserable than he was now.*

Loving Mariah Eller was the best thing that had happened to him in his entire life. She made him laugh as well as think, she challenged his assumptions and gave him a reason to wake up in the morning. He truly *loved* her. And he'd been too afraid of the damnable "consequences" to tell her that. Even after she'd bared her soul to him. Even after she'd given him all the love and passion she possessed. Even after she'd opened his eyes and heart and life to the possibilities all around him.

What the hell was wrong with him?

Leaving the nearly full bottle on the clubroom table, he stalked out into the street and began to walk. Professor Jamison's words came back to him: a man has obligations to himself as well as to his country and his family. Mariah's observations followed close behind: he needed someone to encourage him to rebel, to try new things, to live life on his own terms instead of his family's. No truer words were ever spoken. And the "someone" he needed was Mariah.

She was the one who saw not only the man he was, but the man he could someday be. And she loved both. If he didn't make her his, legally and morally, he would be consigning himself to a life half lived in the service of others' ambitions and desires.

When he came to his senses some time later, he found himself back at Claridge's. He looked up at the lights coming from the upstairs windows and his heart beat faster at the thought that she might be there. He knew then that his heart would always beat faster at the prospect of her presence.

What the devil was he waiting for?

He practically leapt over the desk to get his key, then took the steps two at a time to her room. Her door was locked. She wasn't there. The look in her eyes as Bertie had led her away returned to haunt him. He should have spoken up…should have done something…

Stomach in knots, he headed for his own room and found the door ajar. Bracing, he entered and slammed the door so hard that it bounced.

"Well, Jack, you've gotten yourself into a real mess this time."

He straightened slowly from his defensive stance, scowling at the two men waiting for him by the hearth: the canny Baron Marchant and Jack's eldest brother, Jared the Perfect.

"You're supposed to be procuring a mistress, not poaching one," Jared continued, unfolding his tall frame from a low stool by the hearth.

"What the hell are you doing here?" Jack demanded of his brother, then glowered at Marchant, guessing he was responsible.

"Saving your ungrateful arse," Jared said irritably. "You should be kissing Marchant's boots for alerting me to this insanity."

"You can't deny it, Jack," Marchant charged. "I saw you with her."

So Marchant had seen them together and gone to fetch his brother.

"You were sent to marry off the widow and decided to sample the goods yourself," Jared snapped. "Stupid, but not fatal. I'm here to fix things so that the prince never finds out what an idiot you've been."

"Go home, Jared," Jack said quietly, feeling old angers rising. "This is none of your business."

"Whatever affects my family's reputation *is* my business, little brother. I won't have you bringing the enmity of king and crown down upon our family just so you can have a roll in the hay with one of Bertie's sluts."

"Shut up, Jared." Jack's muscles coiled. "You don't know what—or who—you're talking about."

Jared looked to Marchant, who was indignation personified. "Oh, I think I have a fair picture. I've been there myself, remember? The hunting trip. The nubile widow. It's Bertie's stock in trade. He has a rare talent for sniffing out women with more ambition than virtue."

"You don't know the first thing about her," Jack said, quieting as he worked to control his anger. Jared stalked closer.

"So now you're the tart's champion and defender? Oh, God—don't tell me." Jared clapped his hand to his forehead. "You've gone and fallen for the chit. You're in *love,* is that it?"

"I'm telling you, Jared, leave it. Go home to your wife and children. I'll handle this my way."

"She's using you," Jared snarled. "She's a common trollop who wants someone who can pay the bills when Bertie throws her over."

"Get out," Jack snarled. "Before I throw you out!"

He grabbed Jared's arm to drag him to the door, and the next instant, they were grappling, gouging, knocking over chairs and banging into a sideboard, sending crockery crashing.

# 19

THE PRINCE OF WALES sat in his coach outside Claridge's, watching "Dandy" escort Mariah Eller into the hotel and feeling a twinge of relief. The dapper Dandy had been instructed to wait until she reached her rooms, then to see if Jack was in his room and bring him out for a talk with Bertie.

"She honestly proposed marrying St. Lawrence?" Jack Sprat, seated across from Bertie, reacted to the prince's news with a loosened jaw that made his thin, dolorous face look even longer. "Iron Jack?"

"Doesn't know him like we do, eh, Avery?" Bertie shook his head. "Thinks she can mold him into something 'suitable.'"

"Humph. Not unless she's got a hammer and tongs up her skirts." Sprat sat forward to look out as Bertie sat back. "Never seen a man with more steel in his spine."

"Twice the man his brothers were. Dependable as sunrise. Now and again comes up with a remark that lets you know those still waters run plenty deep." Bertie tapped his temple. "Keeps his thoughts close, though."

"Thinks too much," Sprat diagnosed. "Not good for a man."

"He's seen me to my bed more times than I care to remember." The future king turned somber. "Been a loyal and considerate fellow on all accounts. I'd hate to see him come to a bad end over a woman."

"Still and all, she is a beauty," Sprat ruminated. "And witty."

"Too clever by half. Managed to dispense with the list in order to set her sights on him. Scheming minx. Not that I don't admire ambition in a woman…just not in a mistress."

"So, you've gone off her then?"

"I'll see what Jack has to say." Bertie sighed sharply. "If I do go forward with her, it will be short. Don't sleep well beside a clever woman. Never have."

"Jack! Stop!"

Mariah rushed into Jack's room to intervene, but had to dodge the grappling men to avoid being knocked down. "Stop it, Jack—please!"

Her presence registered and his slackening hold gave his opponent space to wedge in a blow. His head snapped back and he staggered but kept his feet. She made for him, but he waved her back and charged the man again, this time landing a punch that knocked his opponent to his knees. She managed to grab him by the coat and pull him back toward the door.

"What's going on, Jack? Who is this?"

"My brother…the honorable Jared St. Lawrence…come to see I don't embarrass the family," Jack said, panting as he wiped blood from his cheek.

Mariah recognized the similarity in size and coloring between the two men as Jared shoved to his feet and reached for his handkerchief, eyes blazing. But there the similarities stopped. Jared was Jack carved out of pure flint.

"This must be Bertie's trull," he said, raking her with a hostile glare.

"Her name is Mariah Eller. Widow of Sir Mason Eller." Jack pulled her against his side. "Soon to be my wife."

"For God's sake, Jack!" Marchant stepped forward, mopping his brow. "She's already Bertie's mistress, for all intents and purposes. He expects to have her in his bed a week from now."

Horror filled Mariah as Jack's brother turned a scathing look on her. Jack's friends…his family…Bertie…they all thought the worst of her. How long would it be before their common opinion overwhelmed Jack's reputation and prospects and slowly poisoned him against her?

Even as her heart was sinking, Jack put an arm around her and pulled her against his side. He was saying something about what Jared and the baron could do with— Wait. What was it he said a minute ago? She was going to be his wife?

She tried to get him to talk to her, but he ushered her forcefully out the door and toward her room. She caught sight of Mercy standing a few doors down, wearing her nightcap, quilted gown and a thick shawl.

"Get your mantle and a cloak for Mercy," Jack said as they reached Mariah's door. "She's coming with us."

"Coming where?" Trying to resist him was like trying to halt a locomotive engine with a full head of steam. "Tell me what you're—"

"For once, just do as I ask, Mariah," he said, ignoring the protests of his brother and Marchant spilling into the hall behind them. "I've had enough of people telling me what's what tonight."

He pulled her and Mercy with him down the stairs and through the lobby to order the night doorman to find them a cab, a wagon—anything with wheels. He was so intent on the rush of rebellion in his veins that he failed to see the familiar figure of Jack A. Dandy lounging by the reception desk or to notice the way the fellow snapped to attention at the sight of them.

WAITING across the street, Bertie and Sprat saw the doorman rush out of the hotel and give two short, sharp blasts of his whistle, summoning a growler. But after a look up and down the street, spotting none of the four-seater cabs, he blew a single sharp blast and waved on a smaller Hansom that was waiting down the block.

As the doorman rushed back to the lobby, the doors burst open and Jack and Mariah Eller emerged, dragging an old woman with them. The three crowded into the two-seater and took off at a fierce clip.

While they were staring after the cab, Dandy came running out and Sprat opened the door to admit him.

"What in hell's going on?" Bertie demanded. "Where is he off to?"

"No…idea," Dandy wheezed, trying to catch his breath. "I delivered her, she got her key…I gave her time to get to her room. I was starting up to fetch Jack for you when I heard some kind of a ruckus and he came rushing down with her and some old woman."

"What's the damned idiot doing? Where would he be going at this hour?" Bertie growled in frustration. "I'm going to bloody well find out!" Seizing the impulse of the moment, he stuck his head out the window and ordered his driver, "Follow that cab!"

INSIDE THE Hansom, they were so crowded they could hardly breathe until Jack pulled Mariah onto his lap and wrapped both arms around her. Mercy gave several "tsk's" at the liberty he took with her mistress, but she was too grateful for the room and too busy holding her cloak closed against the cold air coming through the open cab front to complain.

"It won't take long, I promise," he said, running his eyes and hands frantically over Mariah. "Are you all right? Bertie didn't—"

"He was a gentleman." She steadied herself against the

back of the cab seat, turning her shoulder to the wind. "Jack, what happened back there with the baron and your brother?"

"Apparently Marchant saw us in the lobby last night and decided something was going on between us. He fetched my brother to knock some sense into me." His voice hardened. "Never been a successful tactic with me, the frontal assault."

"Jack, I have to tell you—" His fingers to her lips stopped her.

"No, Butterfly, *I* have to tell *you*—" he tossed Mercy a close-your-ears look "—what I should have said days ago." His throat tightened. "I love you. With everything in me. With all that I've got." He stroked her cheek and pulled her dark, luminous gaze into his. "Which may not be much after tonight, but it's all yours. I love you. I can't say it any better." He felt the softening in her frame and pulled her tight against him, holding her fiercely. "I nearly lost my mind when Bertie spirited you away. I was damned close to striking the future king of Britain."

"Ye were with the *prince?*" Mercy gaped at her, then scowled at him. "Ye might 'ave told a body."

"I wasn't exactly thinking straight," he said to both women. "Then I realized, watching him walk away with you, that I don't ever want to lose you. Not even just for a stroll. Not even to my future king."

Mariah's eyes shimmered in the flashes of streetlight.

"Stop there, Jack," she said, taking his face between trembling hands. "It's enough to have you say that you love me." Tears filled her eyes and voice. "I'll cherish that always. But your brother is right. I never fully realized what it might do— you can't ruin yourself on my account."

"A little late to worry about that, isn't it? You've knocked my life arse over teakettle, seven different ways. But the thought of not seeing you, not touching you, not hearing your laugh or breathing your scent is unbearable. I want you in my life, my bed, my heart. I want to laugh with you and celebrate Christmases with you and pick out new hats with you. God willing, I want to have children with you and grow old with you…and read every book in old Mason's scandalous library with you."

Tears rolled down her cheeks at the hope, the love in his eyes. She laid her forehead against his and closed her eyes, wanting nothing more than to embrace the joy battering the "sensible" barriers in her heart.

"Marry me, Mariah, and make me the happiest crazy man in Britain."

She lifted her head to look at him.

"If I marry you, the prince will—"

"Have to look for another mistress? Absolutely. Discover that not even princes get their way all the time? He could use a reminder now and again." He ran his hands up her shoulders to cradle her face. "There are a thousand reasons against it, Butterfly, and only one for it. But that one—the love we feel for each other—outweighs every damned objection you and I and the rest of the world could ever come up with against it.

"Marry me, Mariah. *Make me yours.*"

Make him hers? Take him into her life as she had into her heart? The fact that he thought he had to ask said volumes about his respect for her.

"Yes. Oh, yes!" She flung her arms around his neck and sank into his hungry kiss with all the joy and passion she possessed. From across the coach came a whimper and a sniffle.

"Good work, sarr." Mercy's voice was choked with emotion. "It were touch an' go there for a bit, but ye got 'er done."

The cab stopped outside the vicarage of St. Thea the Divine

Church in the south of Knightsbridge. A single gas lamp provided light for the steps and front doors. Jack put his arm around Mariah as they waited for someone to answer their knock. A bluff, hale-looking blond fellow in a cassock and Anglican split collar opened the door and stood squinting at them in surprise.

"Jack St. Lawrence?" The vicar half smiled, looking confused.

"Nathan—thank God you're still posted here. I need your help."

"Of course, Jack." The clergyman stepped back, making room for them. "Whatever I can do."

Jack's countenance changed as he broke into a beaming smile.

"We need someone to marry us. Tonight."

The good vicar took in their glowing faces and close embrace.

"I think you'd better come in."

He led them into a cozy parlor, where the coals in the grate had already been banked for the night. A petite dark-haired woman wearing a night-braid and a warm robe appeared behind them.

"I heard voices. What is it, Nathan?" she asked, wiping sleep from her luminous brown eyes.

"You caught me up late finishing a sermon," the vicar said. "This is my wife, Kristine." He beckoned to her and she went to settle in the crook of his arm. "This is Jack St. Lawrence, dear…the fellow I used to count on to keep me from being hacked mercilessly in football matches at school. He's…here for a wedding."

"This is my bride, Mariah Eller," Jack said. "Mariah, this is Father Nathan Lord. We were at Rugby together as boys."

"Just Nathan, please…if you don't mind," Nathan said.

"Congratulations." Kristine's face lighted as she embraced

Mariah and wished her many years of happiness and a house filled with healthy children. "I'll go light the candles."

"But, Kristine—" Nathan began.

She reached for a shawl and was out the door before he could stop her. He sighed.

"She's often asked to prepare the church and stand in as a witness. It seems she never tires of weddings." Then he took Jack aside for a moment. "There is, however, a potential obstacle. I can't read the vows, Jack, if it is not to be a legal and binding marriage. We must have a license."

"No problem." Jack reached into his coat pocket and pulled out the envelope that had seared itself into his consciousness. "A special license. A friend secured it from the Bishop of London for me—" he glanced at Mariah with a speaking look "—thinking I might need it on short notice."

Father Nathan opened it and looked it over, eyes widening. "You always did have influential friends, Jack." He frowned. "Mariah's name is here but yours is not."

"That's easily remedied." Jack took the paper, smoothed it out on the side table and filled in his own name and signature. Afterward Mariah signed with trembling hands and then asked Mercy to stand up with her. The old servant nodded through a drizzle of tears.

When the paperwork was done, Jack and Mariah followed Nathan through the open walkway into a chilly stone sanctuary warmed by two banks of glowing tapers. After a few instructions, they took their places before the chancel railing in the fragrant glow of beeswax candles, holding hands and feeling their hearts racing.

As Father Nathan directed them, they traded promises of faith and fidelity, agreeing to love, comfort, and support each other in sickness and health, riches and poverty, and through good times and bad. Halfway through the ceremony a toddler in a nightgown came stumbling into the sanctuary, rubbing his eyes. Kristine picked him up in her shawl and patted him to send him back to sleep.

Then came those blessed words: "I pronounce you husband and wife."

Jack not only kissed Mariah afterward but picked her up and swung her around as he did so. She wrapped her arms around his neck, absorbing the moment, letting her laughter mingle with his. When he set her back on her feet, she caught both his gaze and his heart with her smile.

"There's no turning back now," she said, glowing.

"You're mine at last." His voice lowered but still carried all the way to the back of the church. "And no matter what happens tomorrow and the day after, I am yours."

FATHER NATHAN and Kristine invited them into the rectory for a glass of wine and some cake which they gladly accepted. Soon the church was quiet enough that whispers could be heard at the back, in the darkened narthex.

"Never thought to see such a thing in this life," Sprat said in a loud whisper, looking at his equally stunned companions.

"Iron Jack as giddy as a schoolgirl," Dandy added, disillusioned.

"She's bewitched him," Bertie said, scowling. "Conniving little muff. Don't know how the hell she did it, but it's clear she did. He marched right up of his own free will and spoke vows with her. Used the special license I provided for her for himself! I've half a mind to make her live up to our agreement. At least once. Just to teach 'em a lesson."

The three tiptoed back to the shadow-cloaked entrance, where Jack A. Dandy paused while opening the front doors.

"But, what if it's real?" he said. "I mean, it *could* be a love match. Such things are known to happen."

Sprat looked quite horrified. "Good God."

Bertie gave him a smack on the arm. "You're in a church, you horse's arse. And with me." When Sprat looked mystified, he snarled. "The next head of the Church of England?"

"Deepest pardon, Highness." Sprat shriveled. Bertie picked the oddest times to insist on ecclesiastical niceties.

"They look *happy*," Dandy persisted. "You think perhaps they've fallen in love?"

Bertie looked at the pair of them as if unable to believe his ears.

"You're going dotty in your advancing years, the both of you." He pushed past them to exit and then paused outside to make certain Jack's party was still in the rectory. Beckoning for his coach, he muttered, "Love. Humph. You should have heard her talking about him earlier…about how she'd mold him and make him over into…"

An ugly thought struck him as his footman jumped down to open the door and unfold the carriage steps for him.

"She is a clever slip of muslin. It's possible she purposefully…"

"She what, Highness?" Dandy asked, leaning closer.

"Couldn't be." Bertie grabbed the door and hoisted his bulk into the carriage. "No woman in her right mind would turn down the chance to make her fortune in a prince's bed."

Sprat and Dandy looked at each other and chorused, "Absolutely not."

Bertie was clearly out of sorts as he chewed on what to do all the way back to St. James Palace. He sometimes spent nights there so that his manly "recreations" wouldn't disturb his wife at Marlborough House.

By the time they reached St. James, he had what he fancied to be a clever plan. A pity he couldn't test its soundness against the wits of one of the few men he could count on to tell him the truth: Jack St. Lawrence.

"Cranmer," he called Jack A. Dandy to attention as they disembarked within the walls of St. James. "Find me a cart-load of roses, some champagne and a diamond brooch the size of a walnut. Wake people up if you have to—we don't hand out those damned royal warrants for nothing. Have them all delivered to *her* at Claridge's, first thing tomorrow morning." He turned to Sprat. "You, Avery…find me Edgar Marchant. Sober. I don't care if you have to turn out every card room in club land."

# 20

MARIAH SAT on Jack's lap on the way back to Claridge's in the two-seater cab he flagged down on the Brompton Road. Mercy, done in by three glasses of wine and two pieces of cake, was dead to the world, so they were virtually alone. Mariah studied the slope of his nose, the strength of his jaw, and the softness of his dark hair. Every aspect of him pleased her, roused her, completed her. How could she be so lucky?

"I can hardly believe we're married." She buried her face in the crook of his neck and breathed in his warmth. "Tomorrow we get to wake up together, after sleeping in the same bed."

"Not before noon, however," he whispered, kissing her temple, her cheek and her throat as she offered them to him. "Because tonight I intend to keep you up late, ravishing you."

"*Ravishing*...what a lovely word," she whispered, then gasped quietly as his hand slipped beneath her jacket. "Ohhh." She closed her eyes and sucked in a breath as his fingers skimmed her breast above her corset. "Shall I try on my new dressing gowns for you?"

He chuckled. "I doubt you'll have time," he whispered, his hot breath sending trickles of excitement through her. "I'm more in the mood for claiming and devouring."

"Devouring?" she murmured. The word itself sent heat pouring into her sex. "Like this?" She nibbled his lip.

"Mmm."

"Or this?" She tongued his ear and sucked his earlobe.

"Just like that," he said, his voice dropping to a frayed rasp.

The minute the cab stopped at the hotel doors, he shifted her off his lap and sprang out to collect the doorman for help in delivering Mercy safely to her bed. Mariah went ahead to her room and stood in the dark, watching the dull glow of light from the hearth and realizing the passage that was taking place in her life. From widow to wife. From death and mourning into life and celebration.

The door latch snicked once, then a second time, and she held her breath. But instead of encircling her waist with his arms, he moved around to face her. In the dimness, his features looked taut and hungry; his eyes glowed the way they had that first night in Bertie's room.

She began to remove her jacket, staring into those hypnotic golden eyes. He gave a deliciously wicked laugh and brushed her hands away to remove her clothes himself. When she stood in corset, knickers and stockings, atop a puddle of skirts and petticoats, he picked her up and swept her back against the wall by the door, pinning her there with his body.

"This—" his voice was ragged and demanding "—is what I wanted to do to you that first night."

With exquisite deliberation, he planted his hands on the wall on either side of her and began to rub his body against hers. Every movement was a revelation, every angle and position an avenue to fresh, untried pleasure. She planted her hands just beneath his, as she had that first night. Soon her nipples had popped free of her corset and he rubbed every part of him against them…face, lips, tongue, chest, ribs. She was vibrating like a violin string by the time he paused to enjoy her response.

"If you're going to ravish me," she said hoarsely, "get on with it."

With a laugh he began to do just that, kissing, tonguing, nipping…until she was incandescent with desire. By the time she reached for his trousers, he allowed her to guide him and soon supported her with his arms and thighs. When she climaxed, he took release as well and they collapsed together against the wall, waiting for the strength to move to the bed. She kissed his burning ears and rumpled his hair.

"You know, we might have saved a lot of time and trouble if you *had* done this to me that first night."

With a teasing growl, he picked her up and carried her to the bed. This time her corset and knickers came completely off. But the stockings, as always, stayed on.

The next morning, the early sunlight turned Jack's big body to gold as it sprawled over her and the bed. He looked a little civilized and a little barbaric, and a whole lot desirable. He was hers.

She slipped from under his arm and leg and stretched, feeling small, suggestive aches from the night's exertions. A bath, she wanted a warm bath. Sliding from the bed, she padded into the bathing room, lighted the water heater, and prepared for a bath. Just as she was adjusting the final temperature of the water, she heard a tapping at their outer door.

Fearing it would wake Jack, she quickly donned her dressing gown and went to answer it. Outside stood every porter in the hotel, the manager, and even a couple of the morning-room attendants, all bearing large baskets of roses…big, gorgeous, extravagant roses in red, pink and white. She admitted them, holding a finger to her lips to insist on quiet. Behind them, on a rolling cart draped with linen, came an exotic display of fresh oranges and raspberries, buttery French madeleines and gâteau and champagne.

She was overwhelmed at the largess. Her heart swelled as she went from one fabulous bouquet to another, growing intoxicated on the heavenly scents. When the room was cleared of extraneous people, she grabbed an orange and peeled it, then carried it to the bed. She waved it under Jack's nose and he smiled lazily, keeping his eyes shut. With some coaxing he finally opened his mouth and nibbled it.

"Delicious." Groaning, he pushed up onto his elbow and looked around the room in amazement. "What's all this?"

"As if you don't know," she said, giving him an enormous hug.

"This is marvelous," he said, sitting up and raking his hands through his hair. He rubbed his eyes and looked again. "Who are they from?"

"What a tease," she chided. "You'll have all the thanks you can bear after I've had a warm soak and something to eat. I have to keep up my strength for—"

She halted in the midst of carrying a perfect red rose to him on the bed, realizing he truly was confused.

"You didn't send them?" She felt her stomach sink.

"I would have loved surprising you with such a grand gesture, Butterfly. But when would I have had time to arrange it?"

She turned to look at all the flowers and the tea cart. For the first time she noticed an envelope on it addressed to My Lovely Mariah.

Her knees weakened as she picked it up, dreading what she would find inside. The signature of the note confirmed her worst fear.

"It's Bertie," she said without looking up. She couldn't bear to see Jack's face. "They're from him. He asks that I join him tonight for an evening of games and entertainments at The Wetherington Assembly Rooms."

He was out of the bed in a heartbeat and reaching for the note. As he read it, he reddened all the way to the roots of his hair.

"It's an exclusive club," he told her, his mouth tensing into a grim line. "Lots of gambling and drinking and fast company."

"What do I do?" She hadn't expected such trouble so soon.

"What do *we* do?" he corrected her, taking her into his arms. "We're in this marriage, this life together, remember? We'll figure it out together."

He kissed her tenderly and promised he'd be back as soon as he'd gotten some fresh clothes from his room.

She set the note back on the table of luscious food and noticed in the center of that extravagant display a small velvet box. With unsteady hands she picked it up, opened it, and nearly fainted. There was an oval diamond brooch inside that shone in the morning light like a small sun. It had to be worth a fortune. Staggering back to collapse on the bed, she stared at it in horror.

A gift from Bertie to his mistress.

A gift worth a king's ransom.

Or a woman's virtue.

She looked around at the roses and champagne and back at the diamonds. It was a bribe. A not-so-subtle way of letting her know that she'd been claimed and paid for.

And what did it mean that he'd sent such things after she'd proposed marrying Jack? That he intended to let her wed Jack and then claim her as his mistress anyway? Could he have so little regard for Jack's honor and her own moral standards? It would crush Jack to know Bertie could treat him so. Feeling sick, she clicked the box closed, carried it into the bathroom, and tucked it into a stack of towels.

A moment later, the door reopened and she hurried out to find Jack holding a familiar-looking vellum envelope and handwritten invitation.

"I got one, too," he said. "The same time, the same place."

"We have to go, don't we?"

He nodded. "So, we'll go." He pulled her into his arms, taking strength from her and giving it back in equal measure. "And we'll tell him the truth."

THE WETHERINGTON ASSEMBLY ROOMS were actually a single mansion in the west end of London, in an area of townhomes belonging to the wealthy. Built originally by a shirttail royal, it had been sold for debts and had traded hands until it was suggested as a replacement for the gaming houses and deteriorating pleasure gardens being closed in other parts of the city.

The Wetherington never attained or aspired to the respectability of an Almack's. It developed instead a more dangerous and alluring cachet as the sporting ground of people of fashion who had secrets to keep and money to wager. It was a place where men could be seen openly with their mistresses and gaming buffs could find stakes high enough to tempt jaded palates.

The prince arrived early, claimed the old library—now a gentlemen's smoking room—as his base for the evening, and settled in to wait. It wasn't long before Sprat arrived with Baron Marchant in hand.

"There you are." Bertie waved Marchant to a seat on one of the leather sofas and offered him a cigar. There was an edge about the west-country baron tonight, and a tightness about his red-rimmed eyes that Bertie noted without comment.

"Tell me how your special project is going, Edgar." He rubbed his hands together in a show of eagerness. "You know, the one I asked you and Jack St. Lawrence to handle a fortnight back."

"Actually…" Marchant looked as if his collar was bothering him. "I haven't spoken to St. Lawrence since I reported our success to you more than a week ago. I left the lady in his care. I'm sure all has gone well and the lady will be ready to receive you soon."

Bertie casually rolled the ash from his cigar into a cut-glass tray. "You haven't checked to see how things are going?" he asked.

Marchant shrugged, choosing his words carefully.

"I presume that Jack has handled it with his customary thoroughness and dispatch."

"I have heard rumors that the lady is already in London. That St. Lawrence brought her here and has been seen out and about with her."

"Truly?" Marchant sat straighter, feigning surprise. "I had no idea."

"*No* idea?" Bertie smiled one of his affable but totally inscrutable smiles…the sort that men who knew him well dreaded.

A door opened on the far side of the room to reveal Jared St. Lawrence standing outside, his face ruddy with contained outrage. Further pretense was useless. With a defensive huff, Marchant confessed.

"I left him with instructions to see her wedded within two weeks, as I reported to you. The next thing, I knew, he was in London with her. And I saw them together. At Claridge's. Looking chummy."

"How 'chummy'?" Bertie demanded.

"It was a bollocks-up disaster." Marchant's words were not so carefully chosen now. "I asked his brother to help me talk some sense into him. I thought he would see reason and you would never—" He halted, realizing his misstep, but Bertie finished for him.

"Never know that he had 'been there before me'?" Bertie said with ice in his eyes. "Edgar, you and I have had our ups and downs. I've always made allowances for your peccadilloes because you were often amusing and sometimes earnest." Bertie stubbed out his cigar and rose. "But a prince must be certain of whom he can and cannot trust."

When he turned his back and strolled to one of the book-shelves to peruse the titles, Marchant staggered to his feet and looked to Sprat and Dandy for help. Neither man would meet his gaze. The prince's sufferance had run out. Marchant tugged down his vest, red-faced, and strode out.

Bertie took a book off the shelf and spoke to Jack's brother while examining the antique leather binding.

"Jared, my boy, go have a bit of fun. You look like you could use it."

When the door closed behind Jack's brother, Bertie turned back to Sprat and Dandy.

"Is she here?"

"Just arrived. Jack is here, too. They arrived together."

"Is she wearing it?" Bertie asked.

"I didn't see it," Sprat said, adding glumly, "but that doesn't mean much. My eyes aren't what they used to be."

"Give them a few minutes, and then bring her to me. *Alone.*"

# 21

THE GASLIGHT and the banks of candles that illuminated the main salons and card rooms of the Wetherington gave the place a warm, romantic glow. Music from a string ensemble floated through the halls with the guests, lively and spirited and transitory. The well-heeled patrons were dressed in the latest fashions, some laden with jewels and others, like Mariah Eller St. Lawrence, sparkling without the aid of gems.

As she arrived, wearing a midnight-blue dinner gown adorned with perfect white roses, wearing white roses in her upswept hair, she created a stir. Then her escort was recognized and rumors began to fly in earnest. Jack St. Lawrence, one of Bertie's beloved St. Lawrences, was with a tantalizing beauty that no one seemed to know. When it was learned that the lady was Iron Jack's wife, gossip reached a fevered pitch.

Mercifully, Mariah understood little of the interest swirling around her. The faces, introductions and best wishes on her recent nuptials melted into a blur, but every burst of laughter or crash of a falling glass made her flinch and look up, half expecting to see Bertie bearing down on them. Jack, battling his own tensions, never failed to squeeze her hand and give her a reassuring smile. She was grateful for his strength at her side and tried to lend him whatever support she could.

Watching for and dreading Bertie's appearance, she was

unprepared for handsomely dressed Jack A. Dandy to suddenly appear at her side and insist on escorting her to see a "friend." Dandy relayed to Jack the prince's explicit instructions: he would see Mariah *alone*.

Torn between protectiveness and possessiveness, Jack followed them like a big, ineffectual shadow. Should he barge in with her to face Bertie with the truth, or trust that Bertie would behave honorably and listen to her? The next moment, his thoughts shamed him. Bertie's honor, once engaged, was never in question. It was Bertie's forgiveness that left significant room for doubt. What would he do when he learned they were married and that Jack didn't intend to share her with his prince?

When they arrived at the library doors, Dandy advised Jack to stay outside until he was summoned. But it was only when Mariah kissed his cheek and assured him that she was all right to go in alone that he relented and let Dandy usher her inside.

THE DOORS closing behind Mariah sounded like the snapping jaws of a steel trap. She found herself in what appeared to be a library furnished with shelves laden with books and curiosities, a desk, chairs and lamps for reading. At the center of this elegant web sat the Prince of Wales, dressed in evening clothes and looking august and intimidating.

As Dandy bowed and exited through a side door, Bertie rose and extended a hand. "My dear, you look enchanting. The male population of London will lie at your feet before the night is out."

"You are too kind, Your Highness." She prayed he couldn't feel how icy her hands were through her gloves. "But I am not a greedy woman. One man is quite enough for me."

"Is it now?" Bertie raised an eyebrow. "Then you are a rare specimen of femininity indeed."

She allowed him to lead her to the leather sofa, but declined to sit.

"I must thank you for the gift of this morning," she said. "It was as unexpected as it was extravagant. I wear it to honor your generosity."

He studied her fashionably low-cut bodice and fetching use of roses.

"But, I believe something is missing. Was there not something a bit more eye-catching than just pretty flowers?"

She met the question in his gaze straight on.

"It is not missing, Highness. It is here." She opened her small reticule and removed the diamond brooch, relieved to have brought it thus far without Jack's knowledge. She reached for the prince's hand and placed it in his palm, closing his fingers around it.

"What is this?" He looked at it and then at her in disbelief.

"I cannot accept it. It would be dishonorable of me to take such a gift. And even more dishonorable to keep knowledge of it from my husband."

"You've married?" Bertie seemed startled. "Since yesterday?"

"Last night."

"So that is it." He scowled, looking her over. "I thought there was something different about you."

"Marriage does change a body, Highness," she said softly. "I pray it won't displease you to hear that my partner in that sacrament is Jack St. Lawrence. Your Jack." She felt his stare like rays of sun piercing her liberally exposed skin. "Now my Jack, too."

His frown deepened, then he turned and stalked away, leaving her to clasp her hands and hold her breath. His silence outlasted her.

"I have a confession to make, Your Highness," she said finally.

"Yes?" He didn't turn.

"I married Jack not because I had to, but because I wanted to. I care very much for him." Her throat tightened such that she had to pause for a moment. "And it is because I love and honor him…and I wish to honor and esteem you…that I must ask you to release me from our agreement. I cannot be both his wife and your mistress."

He turned to look her up and down, then began to pace, appearing troubled, irritable and uncertain. Then he stopped and pointed to the sofa.

"Sit. And explain to me exactly how this betrayal occurred."

Her knees buckled. She hit the sofa with her bottom, feeling jarred.

"If it was a betrayal, the fault was mine. I was unhappy about being coerced into being your paramour and insisted on choosing my husband."

"Coerced?" Bertie propped his fists on his waist. "Good God."

"I felt I had no choice. The baron said some debts I had incurred on behalf of my inn would be called due if I did not submit to you."

"Submit? Good Lord—you make me sound like a pillaging Hun!"

"Then Jack was assigned to see me married off. I insisted on seeing the men on his list with my own eyes and found them exactly as I described them to you last night. Poor Jack…his frustration was monumental. He's a very logical and rational man. He couldn't fault my refusal of them. They were so unsuitable. Yet, he was desperate to be rid of me. I'm afraid I wasn't disposed to make his task any easier than mine," she continued. "I was hard on him at times."

"Oh?" He was openly skeptical. "How?"

"Well, he was straightforward about what you might expect from me, so I felt it only fair to be as blunt with him about my expectations for a husband." She took a shuddery breath. "He was squeamish about my explicitness. And appalled by my *list*."

"What 'list'?" His eyes and mouth both tightened.

"Qualities I would accept in a husband. I insisted we come to London to find someone who would meet them."

"You truly intended to marry?"

"I was resigned to it, Highness."

He stared at her as if having difficulty with the notion of anyone being "resigned" to amorous pursuits with him.

"Damn and blast me," he said, searching her face, her eyes.

She wilted a bit under that scrutiny. He was a formidable presence, for all his princely ways. It was a relief when he looked away.

"The thing is, Highness, I discovered he met every criterion on my list. Every one. And then some. He was patient, honorable, respectful… I came to enjoy and then crave his company. He can be quite droll when he wants. And he laughed in all the right places and sometimes teased me."

"Laughed?" Bertie looked away, seeming disturbed by that idea. "Don't think I've ever seen Jack let go that much."

"He has a wonderful, deep, booming laugh, Highness. And when I learned how he had given up his scholarly hopes to serve you, and—"

"Scholarly hopes?"

"His studies at Cambridge. He was asked to stay, you know, and continue his work. Perhaps join the faculty."

"Who told you such a thing?"

"His old professor at Cambridge. Jack's family insisted he leave the college to come and serve you after his elder brother was married."

"I've heard enough." He waved a hand to enforce the command and then rose, looking none too pleased. He paced for a moment in silence as she watched with icy limbs, a dry mouth and a thudding heart.

"You wish me to believe this was all unintended? Just the flow of circumstance?" Bertie said, coming to a halt nearby.

"My wishing you to believe it does not make it any less true, Highness. Jack is the most loyal man you will ever meet. And it was never my intention to give offense, despite my reservations."

Bertie stalked away again, his hands clasped behind his back, looking as though he bore the weight of the world on his shoulders. Then he turned to her.

"Very well, I release you from our agreement…with the understanding that I am released as well. The expenses incurred will now fall to you, madam, as debts to be paid."

She felt the color draining from her face. She looked down at her costly blue silk, which suddenly felt more like a prisoner's shackles than elegant couture. The half smile on his face said he read her reaction well.

"Now that you see the limitations this marriage places on your future, what if I were to give you a second chance to cast your fortunes with me?"

"What?" She pushed to her feet and swayed slightly.

He reached into his pocket and pulled out the diamond brooch.

"Jack's family is ambitious. This could be just the start of a very stylish and luxurious life for you, my dear. And the making of Jack's career. Many men in government have been helped along by wives willing to do their part…in a prince's bed." He held out the brooch with a knowing expression. "We could forget all of this unpleasantness and start again."

Was he serious? Had he heard, believed nothing that she had said?

Her heart sank at the thought of all that was stacked against them—Bertie's disapproval as well as Jack's family's, and now a host of fresh debts that must be paid. Would Jack regret that their marriage had cost him the prince's trust and the financial security and opportunities that came with it?

"You are more than generous, Highness, to offer such an opportunity a second time." She forced herself to stand tall. "But my heart and loyalties are now Jack's. And though I wish to be loyal to my prince, there are things I cannot render to you without being even more disloyal to the one who holds my heart." She felt her face might shatter from the effort her smile required. "I would not, could not betray him in another's bed. Not for all the jewels and riches and palaces in the kingdom."

Abruptly, he strode for the side door, calling for Jack A. Dandy, who appeared in seconds, peering curiously at her.

"Cranmer," he declared, "show Mrs. St. Lawrence around the gaming tables and give her some chips to play." His voice was cool and imperial. "Clearly, she's of a mood to test her luck tonight."

She left the library feeling unsteady and disoriented, glad for the support of Dandy's arm. What had just happened with the prince? Did he believe her? Did he understand that in loving Jack, she meant no disrespect toward him? Was he furious? Would he seek retribution? It unnerved her that she had no more answers now than when she went in to see him.

"Jack," she said quietly, gripping Dandy's arm. "Where is he?"

"He's with the prince," Dandy said, patting her hand as it lay on his arm. "Come now. I'll show you how the betting's done."

# 22

JACK TRIED not to look as if he was pacing outside the library door. He couldn't help feeling he should have shouldered his way in and faced Bertie with her. Several times, he stepped to the door. Twice his fingers actually gripped the knob. They had intended to speak to the prince together to reveal their marriage. Why hadn't he just barged in with her?

When the door finally opened, it was Bertie himself who stood just inside. The prince looked him up and down before ordering him to "close the door behind you."

Bertie settled on the edge of the large mahogany desk and crossed his arms, looking irritable indeed.

"Sit," he commanded, nodding to the chair in front of him.

Jack didn't need to be told that Bertie had heard the truth from Mariah, but the prince's demeanor gave no hint of how he'd taken the news.

"What the hell have you done?" the prince demanded after a moment. "I told you to find her a husband—not marry her yourself! Are you mad?"

"Probably." Jack swallowed hard. Bertie clearly hadn't taken the news well. "Mad as a march hare. But a very happy march hare, Highness."

"Oh, don't give me that 'Highness' nonsense. There's no quicker way to earn a 'sod off' from me, and you know it. How could you, Jack?" His voice and face became thunderous. "You had a bright and promising future ahead of you. The right marriage, a word from me here and there, and you would have been—"

"Condemned to a prosperous, dull, stifling life doing things I never wanted to do," Jack said, fully aware of the risk he took in interrupting.

Bertie was shocked speechless for a moment.

"You mean to say you've been bored and miserable in my company?" he thundered.

"Not at all," Jack protested, leaning forward. "I have greatly enjoyed being part of your hunting circle, and I feel privileged to have been of service to you. But, as an old professor of mine recently reminded me, a man has obligations besides those to his country and family. How can a man do his best for his country and family if there is nothing inside him but duty and obligation? If the whole of his inner self is an empty shell?"

Bertie stared at him, seeming troubled, before stalking away to pick up the antique volume that had interested him earlier.

Jack took a deep breath, watching Bertie, praying his next words would find some resonance in the prince's well-guarded heart.

"Love and passion…curiosity and wonder…joy and hope… there is a whole world of feelings and experiences beyond the satisfaction of loyalty and a duty well done. You, more than all other men, know that to be truly alive, a man must have more than duty in his soul." He rose to face Bertie, who looked down, reacting strongly to the truth of Jack's words.

"For these last three years," Jack continued, "I have given you my loyalty and held your interests above all else. Is it disloyal of me now to want what fills my heart and makes me a better, more complete man?"

Bertie turned enough to search him with rueful eyes.

"Tell me the truth, Jack. Why did you marry her?"

Jack squared his shoulders, praying his words would find their target.

"The truth is, I went to negotiate for a mistress and discovered a woman who couldn't be bought." He gave a pained smile. "I went to find her a husband and found the missing parts of my heart instead. I expected a clever, calculating female and found a warm, intelligent woman who wasn't afraid to speak for herself and others. I married her because I couldn't bear to let her go. She is the half of me I hadn't even known was missing."

"She's a conniving wench," Bertie charged, without much heat.

"That she is." Jack's smile softened.

"She's beguiled you."

"And what a sweet bit of sorcery it's been," Jack agreed, his tension easing.

"She's likely to be the death of your career."

At that, Jack sobered. It took a minute for him to collect himself.

"Any career that required me to renounce the foundation of my heart and the love that sustains me is not likely to hold me for long, anyway."

Bertie wagged his head and, after a moment, shifted his approach.

"What if a prince believes that one of his beloved friends has made a grave and costly mistake? Is he not obligated to set things right?"

"What is *right,* sir?" Jack sensed the change and joined Bertie in a mode of discussion they had often followed. "Is it the outcome that pleases you personally or is it the one that makes for a more harmonious kingdom? Is it the conformity of men's lives to a prince's desires, or is it a prince's acceptance of his people's right to determine their own happiness?

"All princes demand loyalty, as is their right. But a good prince knows how to give loyalty as well as require it. And a wise prince knows and respects the hearts of his people."

Emboldened by the warmth and camaraderie of a hundred nights spent together and dozens of conversations, Jack engaged Bertie's eyes.

"I am your man, Your Highness. I will always be. But there are times I must be my own man as well."

After a moment, Bertie turned back to the book in his hands.

"I appreciate your honesty, Jack. I always have." His voice sounded thick with emotion. "I hope someday you will appreciate mine."

With that, he turned his back and Jack understood he was dismissed.

He rose and strode out, reeling from the unexpected nature of the interview and utterly confounded by Bertie's reaction. Had he been cast aside? Was he now *persona non grata* with the prince?

He hurried from salon to salon, searching for Mariah, and found her in the baccarat room, seated at a table behind several sizeable stacks of playing chips. When he set his hands on her shoulders she jumped and turned with her hand to her throat.

"What happened?" She would have stood, but he prevented her from rising and bent to whisper to her.

"I have no idea. I can't tell if he's furious or disappointed or about to roar 'off with his head.'" He glanced at Dandy, who vacated the chair beside her for him.

"She's uncommonly lucky, this new wife of yours." Dandy grinned.

"I am the one with the real luck, Cranmer." He smiled at her until his gaze finally registered the size of the stacks of chips before her. He sat down with a thud on Dandy's chair. "A-are those all yours?"

"Yes," she said, reaching for his hands, aware of the avid faces of the people crowded around the table. "I seem to have a knack for it. I mean, the game just requires doing a few sums and then holding your breath as the cards are dealt. See?"

Even as he watched, she played another hand, then another, raking in an astonishing pile of chips each time. The small crowd that had gathered in the gaming room grew with each winning hand she played. For a moment their precarious position was eclipsed by the surprise of such a financial windfall. She smiled at him and he chuckled, shaking his head.

"I should have known. If anyone would have beginner's luck—"

"I suggest you quit while you are ahead, little brother," came a hostile voice over their shoulders.

Jared had worked his way through the spectators and stood behind their chairs, staring down his long, patrician nose. He bent toward Jack and lowered his voice. "Surely you can tell when you're no longer wanted. Save us all the humiliation of Bertie's public cut. Take your tart and leave."

Jack shot to his feet and pushed Jared back from the table, through the ring of spectators. Jared seized his wrists, Jack grabbed Jared's lapels, and suddenly they were shoving and grappling, snarling at each other as they pitched wildly through the crowd.

"Jack—no—please!" Mariah rushed to follow them as excitement erupted through the crowd. Her heart was in her throat as Jack and his brother struggled, evenly matched, faces furious, teeth gritted.

"Well, well. What have we here?" The prince's irate voice cut through the tension, and the spectators parted around Jack and Jared to admit Bertie and his comrades. Sprat and Dandy rushed to haul the men apart, and were soon joined by Jack Ketch and two other distinguished-looking guests. They peeled Jack from his brother's lapels, muttering cautions and demanding the hostility cease. The sight of the Prince of Wales's icy disapproval was enough to cool their tempers and restore some reason.

"A family spat?" Bertie said with all the force of a royal edict. "Come now. We'll have no more of that. Not on such a momentous occasion."

Jack glowered at his brother even as Mariah rushed to his side and seized his arm, holding him back from any further conflict. It took a moment for Bertie's statement to sink in and Jack to look from her to Bertie. She threaded her fingers through his and found him trembling slightly. Their fate was being announced in front of half of London's worldly elite.

"Occasion, Your Highness?" Jack said in choked tones.

"It's not every day one of my St. Lawrences is wedded, now is it? Come, come—a toast is in order. Where the devil is that champagne?"

Mariah looked to Jack in astonishment, finding him equally surprised. The prince was proposing a wedding toast for them? Half an hour ago he seemed ready to declare them traitors and banish them from his sight.

As glasses of the pale, bubbly wine were circulated among the guests, Bertie insinuated himself between Jack and Mariah, clamping an arm around each, giving them both dangerously cheery looks as he held them forcefully at his sides.

"I take special pride in this union," he announced with emphatic good humor that seemed to be aimed at Jared as much as the crowd around them, "since I was partly responsible for bringing it about. As matchmaker, I would be the first to raise a glass and wish the happy couple—" he released Jack long enough to take a glass of the bubbly from a tray "—long life and happiness and prosperity! To Jack St. Lawrence, the new Secretary General of the Office of Patents, and his lovely bride!"

A wave of congratulations and good wishes swept the crowd, above an undercurrent of curiosity and speculation. This was hardly the usual venue for nuptial celebrations, much less announcements of government appointments. And the near brawl between the groom and his brother hinted that there was a juicy bit more to the story than the prince suggested.

Jared scowled in confusion at the glass Jack Sprat shoved into his hand, but under Bertie's pointed stare, joined the toast and drank.

"The Patent Office, Highness?" Jack said, shocked down to his knees.

"You're always studying some new scientific process or investigating machinery of some kind…figuring out how things work. I'm not blind, you know. In three years, I have taken notice." Bertie looked pointedly at Mariah. "And I have it on good authority that you have always had a yen for science and are brilliant at recognizing the value of inventions. Why not put all that passion to work for crown and empire?"

"Why not indeed?" Mariah said, squeezing Jack's arm, grinning.

"Bertie, I'm overwhelmed," Jack stammered. "It's—it's—"

"Perfect for you, I know," Bertie declared with preening satisfaction. "Knowing what people are good for is something *I'm* brilliant at."

Jack barely had a chance to thank Bertie before the prince was pulling the glasses from their hands and dragging them along in his beefy grip.

"I believe, as your prince and benefactor," Bertie said with a wicked glint in his eye, "I should get to see your first dance as man and wife."

"Dance?" Jack dragged him to a halt, looking as if he'd been impaled.

With a wicked laugh, Bertie led them into the broad down-stairs hall, where the musicians ground to a halt at the sight of him. He ordered up a waltz and then motioned the newly-weds onto the clearing floor. Jack tried not to look as sick as he felt as he escorted Mariah out onto the dance floor.

"Damn his hide, he knows how much I hate dancing," Jack muttered as the music started. "This is pure revenge."

She laughed. "Compared to what he might have done, this is easy."

"For you, maybe," he grumbled, trying to catch the beat of the music.

"Yes, for me." She looked up into his tense gaze, drawing him into her smile and into her love. "So, you'll just have to depend on me for help." Her smile broadened. "And isn't that the way it should be?" She laughed and leaned closer to whisper, "It's simple…just 'one, two three'…'one two three.'" She looked up, her eyes shining. "Let the music fill your heart as you fill mine. And we'll be the only people in the room."

With only a few bumps and hesitations, they were soon waltzing around the floor as if they'd been dancing together for years. They were so absorbed in each other they didn't notice Jack Sprat and Jack A. Dandy murmuring with the prince as they watched.

"So, you think it's the real thing, then?" Sprat asked, watching them.

"As best I can determine. Never seen a woman part with diamonds unless she figured she was getting something a helluva lot more valuable in return. And you should have heard them defending each other. Look at them—" Bertie's voice held a hint of disgust. Or perhaps envy. "Glowing like light bulbs." Then he glanced at Dandy. "How much did she win?"

"A good thirty thousand," the Earl of Avery said with a hint of pique. "Didn't need much help from the dealers, either. That woman has the damnedest luck."

"Should set them up nicely. Damn his hide, I'm going to miss that boy." Bertie sighed and looked restlessly around the glittering crowd. A pair of huge brown eyes caught his attention, framed in a dewy face and set above a noteworthy hourglass shape. "Say, who is that prime filly with the Earl of Warwick's party?"

"Oh, that's Warwick's new countess. I believe her name is Frances. Friends call her Daisy."

"Daisy, Daisy," the prince said under his breath as he tugged down his waistcoat and made his way toward her. "How attached are you to your ambitious husband?"

Out on the floor, several couples had finally joined Jack and Mariah as they whirled around and around. But the two of them had developed such an entrancing rhythm that they were largely unaware of their fellow dancers…or of the fact that the prince was no longer watching.

"See?" she said, adoring him. "You're a wonderful dancer."

"With the right partner," he said. "I have a confession to make. I've just developed a new technique."

"What is it?"

"I imagine my gorgeous wife is dancing naked in my arms."

"How innovative of you," she said, slowing, her eyes shining.

"I'm discovering, however, that it has a flaw," he said, slowing, too, and pulling her closer. "Chiefly, the way it makes me want to—"

He came to a dead stop in the middle of the floor, wrapped his arms around her, and kissed her with everything in him. And by the time that kiss was finished, the Iron had melted from Jack's name forever.

# Author's Note

Rest assured that Prince Albert Edward's documented activities support every characteristic I've given him in *Make Me Yours*. He was a troubled youth whose mother made no secret of her dislike for him. He grew up to rebel emphatically against his dolorous, straight-laced mother and the whole cult of "repression as respectability" that she spawned.

"Bertie," as he was known, was notorious as a womanizer and did indeed possess the quirk of carrying on affairs with only married women. As portrayed in the book, the idea of gaining favor through sex was commonplace in Victorian times, a well-established route to improving a family's status and connections. Noblemen did indeed encourage their wives to "indulge" the prince.

The "Daisy" mentioned at the end of the book was also historical: Frances Maynard Brooke, Countess of Warwick, was the inspiration for the Gay 90's song "Daisy, Daisy" ("a bicycle built for two"). Daisy caused quite a scandal in 1891 by using her affair with Bertie as a cover for her affair with Charles Beresford, one of Bertie's best friends! It became public and the prime minister himself had to intervene to keep the prince from being dragged into the courts. The rupture of the friendship between Bertie and his mistress-poaching friend never healed.

If you're interested in learning more or contacting me, visit BetinaKrahn.com.

\* \* \* \* \*

*Celebrate 60 years of pure reading pleasure
with Harlequin!*

To commemorate the event, Harlequin Intrigue® is thrilled to invite you to the wedding of The Colby Agency's J. T. Baxley and his bride, Eve Mattson.

That is, of course, if J.T. can find the woman who left him at the altar. Considering he's a private investigator for one of the top agencies in the country—the best of the best—that shouldn't be a problem. The real setback is that his bride isn't who she appears to be…and her mysterious past has put them both in danger.

*Enjoy an exclusive glimpse of Debra Webb's
latest addition to*
THE COLBY AGENCY:
ELITE RECONNAISSANCE DIVISION

*THE BRIDE'S SECRETS*

*Available August 2009
from Harlequin Intrigue®.*

The dark figures on the dock were still firing. The bullets cutting through the surface of the water without the warning boom of shots told Eve they were using silencers.

That was to her benefit. Silencers decreased the accuracy of every shot and lessened the range.

She grabbed for the rocks. Scrambled through the darkness. Bumped her knee on a boulder. Cursed.

Burrowing into the waist-deep grass, she kept low and crawled forward. Faster. Pushed harder. Needed as much distance as possible.

Shots pinged on the rocks.

J.T. scrambled alongside her.

He was breathing hard.

They had to stay close to the ground until they reached the next row of warehouses. Even though she was relatively certain they were out of range at this point, she wasn't taking any risks. And she wasn't slowing down.

J.T. had to keep up.

The splat of a bullet hitting the ground next to Eve had her rolling left. Maybe they weren't completely out of range.

She bumped J.T. He grunted.

His injured arm. Dammit. She could apologize later.

Half a dozen more yards.

Almost in the clear.

As she reached the cover of the alley between the first two warehouses she tensed.

Silence.

No pings or splats.

She glanced back at the dock. Deserted.

Time to run.

Her car was parked another block down.

Pushing to her feet, she sprinted forward. The wet bag dragged at her shoulder. She ignored it.

By the time she reached the lot where her car was parked, she had dug the keys from her pocket and hit the fob. Six seconds later she was behind the wheel. She hit the ignition as J.T. collapsed into the passenger seat. Tires squealed as she spun out of the slot.

"What the hell did you do to me?"

From the corner of her eye she watched him shake his head in an attempt to clear it.

He would be pissed when she told him about the tranquilizer.

She'd needed him cooperative until she formulated a plan. A drug-induced state of unconsciousness had been the fastest and most efficient method to ensure his continued solidarity.

"I can't really talk right now." Eve weaved into the right lane as the street widened to four lanes. What she needed was traffic. It was Saturday night—shouldn't be that difficult to find as soon as they were out of the old warehouse district.

A glance in the rearview mirror warned that their unwanted company had caught up.

Sensing her tension, J.T. turned to peer over his left shoulder.

"I hope you have a plan B."

She shot him a look. "There's always plan G." Then she pulled the Glock out of her waistband.

Cutting the steering wheel left, she slid between two

vehicles. Another veer to the right and she'd put several cars between hers and the enemy.

She was betting they wouldn't pull out the firepower in the open like this, but a girl could never be too sure when it came to an unknown enemy.

Deep blending was the way to go.

Two traffic lights ahead the marquee of a movie theater provided exactly the opportunity she was looking for.

The digital numbers on the dash indicated it was just past midnight. Perfect timing. The late movie would be purging its audience into the crowd of teenagers who liked hanging out in the parking lot.

She took a hard right onto the property that sported a twelve-screen theater, numerous fast-food hot spots and a chain superstore. Speeding across the lot, she selected a lane of parking slots. Pulling in as close to the theater entrance as possible, she shut off the engine and reached for her door.

"Let's go."

Thankfully he didn't argue.

Rounding the hood of her car, she shoved the Glock into her bag, then wrapped her arm around J.T.'s and merged into the crowd.

With her free hand she finger-combed her long hair. It was soaked, as were her clothes. The kids she bumped into noticed, gave her death-ray glares.

They just didn't know.

As she and J.T. moved in closer to the building, she grabbed a baseball cap from an innocent bystander. The crowd made it easy. The kid who owned the cap had made it even easier by stuffing the cap bill-first into his waistband at the small of his back.

Pushing through the loitering crowd, she made her way to the side of the building next to the main entrance. She pushed

J.T. against the wall and dropped her bag to the ground. Peeled off her tee and let it fall.

His gaze instantly zeroed in on her breasts, where the cami she wore had glued to her skin like an extra layer. A zing of desire shot through her veins.

Not the time.

With a flick of her wrist she twisted her hair up and clamped the cap atop the blonde mass.

"They're coming," J.T. muttered as he gazed at some point beyond her.

"Yeah, I know." She planted her palms against the wall on either side of him and leaned in. "Keep your eyes open. Let me know when they're inside."

Then she planted her lips on his.

\* \* \* \* \*

*Will J.T. and Eve be caught in the moment?*
*Or will Eve get the chance to reveal all of her secrets?*
*Find out in*
**THE BRIDE'S SECRETS**
*by Debra Webb*
*Available August 2009*
*from Harlequin Intrigue*®

We'll be spotlighting a different series every month throughout 2009 to celebrate our 60th anniversary.

## LOOK FOR
## HARLEQUIN INTRIGUE®
## IN AUGUST!

To commemorate the event, Harlequin Intrigue® is thrilled to invite you to the wedding of the Colby Agency's J.T. Baxley and his bride, Eve Mattson.

**Look for *Colby Agency: Elite Reconnaissance***

# THE BRIDE'S SECRETS
## BY DEBRA WEBB

*Available August 2009*

**www.eHarlequin.com**

HIBPA09

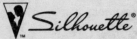

# Romantic
# SUSPENSE

**Sparked by Danger,
Fueled by Passion.**

# CAVANAUGH
# JUSTICE

### The Cavanaughs are back!

### *USA TODAY* bestselling author
# Marie Ferrarella
## *Cavanaugh Pride*

In charge of searching for a serial killer on the loose,
Detective Frank McIntyre has his hands full. When
Detective Julianne White Bear arrives in town searching
for her missing cousin, Frank has to keep the escalating
danger under control while trying to deny the very
real attraction he has for Julianne. Can they keep their
growing feelings under wraps while also handling the
most dangerous case of their careers?

### *Available August wherever books are sold.*

**Visit Silhouette Books at www.eHarlequin.com**

SRS27641

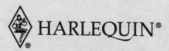

# REQUEST YOUR FREE BOOKS!

## 2 FREE NOVELS PLUS 2 FREE GIFTS!

HARLEQUIN®

*Blaze*

**Red-hot reads!**

**YES!** Please send me 2 FREE Harlequin® Blaze™ novels and my 2 FREE gifts (gifts are worth about $10). After receiving them, if I don't wish to receive any more books, I can return the shipping statement marked "cancel." If I don't cancel, I will receive 6 brand-new novels every month and be billed just $4.24 per book in the U.S. or $4.71 per book in Canada. That's a savings of 15% off the cover price. It's quite a bargain. Shipping and handling is just 50¢ per book.* I understand that accepting the 2 free books and gifts places me under no obligation to buy anything. I can always return a shipment and cancel at any time. Even if I never buy another book, the two free books and gifts are mine to keep forever.

151 HDN EYS2   351 HDN EYTE

| Name | (PLEASE PRINT) | |
|---|---|---|
| Address | | Apt. # |
| City | State/Prov. | Zip/Postal Code |

Signature (if under 18, a parent or guardian must sign)

**Mail to the Harlequin Reader Service:**
**IN U.S.A.:** P.O. Box 1867, Buffalo, NY 14240-1867
**IN CANADA:** P.O. Box 609, Fort Erie, Ontario L2A 5X3

Not valid to current subscribers of Harlequin Blaze books.

**Want to try two free books from another line?**
**Call 1-800-873-8635 or visit www.morefreebooks.com.**

* Terms and prices subject to change without notice. Prices do not include applicable taxes. N.Y. residents add applicable sales tax. Canadian residents will be charged applicable provincial taxes and GST. Offer not valid in Quebec. This offer is limited to one order per household. All orders subject to approval. Credit or debit balances in a customer's account(s) may be offset by any other outstanding balance owed by or to the customer. Please allow 4 to 6 weeks for delivery. Offer available while quantities last.

**Your Privacy:** Harlequin Books is committed to protecting your privacy. Our Privacy Policy is available online at www.eHarlequin.com or upon request from the Reader Service. From time to time we make our lists of customers available to reputable third parties who may have a product or service of interest to you. If you would prefer we not share your name and address, please check here. ☐

# You're invited to join our Tell Harlequin Reader Panel!

By joining our new reader panel you will:

- Receive Harlequin® books—they are FREE and yours to keep with no obligation to purchase anything!
- Participate in fun online surveys
- Exchange opinions and ideas with women just like you
- Have a say in our new book ideas and help us publish the best in women's fiction

*In addition, you will have a chance to win great prizes and receive special gifts!*
*See Web site for details. Some conditions apply.*
*Space is limited.*

To join, visit us at

# www.TellHarlequin.com.

# HARLEQUIN *Blaze*™

## COMING NEXT MONTH

### Available July 28, 2009

### www.eHarlequin.com

HBCNMBPA0709